STORMS
OF THE
PAST

Books by
Jenny Elaine

A SHADY PINES MYSTERY – BOOK 3

STORMS OF THE PAST

JENNY ELAINE

ISBN: 979-8-9853661-2-9

PROLOGUE

29 YEARS EARLIER

With a small suitcase clutched tightly in her hand, Elena walked away from the tiny cabin that had been her home for the last year. Her sneakers made a slight crunching sound as she hurried down the dirt driveway, the damp night air warm against her skin. A thick layer of fog floated among the tops of the trees like a white, lifeless cloud, and the sudden cry of a screech owl as it echoed through the mountains sent chills down Elena's spine.

She didn't like being out at night, especially alone. The solitude in these mountains and the thickness of the trees always frightened her a little. It didn't matter, though. As much as it was breaking her heart to say goodbye, she had no choice but to leave this place.

As Elena neared Black Wolf Lodge, she slowed her steps and listened for the sound of voices. There they were. A mixture of muted tones filled the otherwise quiet night, and Elena bit her bottom lip, wondering how she would get past the lodge without being seen. Taking a deep breath, she stayed as much among the shadows as she could, hoping no one would spot her as she crept toward the road.

It was after midnight, and no guests were staying at the lodge tonight. The owners had just celebrated their official retirement and were gone on a world cruise, leaving their adult children in charge. Frankie and Merrick Levine were now the owners, and Elena could clearly see them in the glow of the back porch light as they sat on the old, creaky rocking chairs. They'd invited their small group of friends, which had never included her, over for one last fling before summer's end. Elena paused for a moment, taking in all the faces. Along with Frankie and Merrick, Elena saw Hudson, Evelyn, and Terrence sitting in a circle. She wondered how it felt now that Jackson was no longer among them. Did they care at all? She'd thought so when he died in that horrible accident over two months ago, but after what she'd overheard earlier today, she wasn't so sure.

"Look, I can't help but be nervous about this. The police are suspicious, and I don't want to go to prison!"

The whispered words had come from the kitchen, where Elena was heading to fix lunch for the lodge's five occupants. She'd stopped at the swinging door and peered carefully inside to see two people standing at the kitchen sink, drinking a glass of sweet tea.

"We won't go to prison if you'll just keep your cool," the second individual replied with a sigh.

"Jackson's death was an accident. End of story."

"His death was no accident; he was murdered, and we both know it. If the police find out, we'll all be implicated."

Elena had made certain to stay hidden as they placed their empty glasses in the sink and left the kitchen. Their conversation, though, remained in her mind for the rest of the day, and she was now almost certain one of them murdered Jackson.

Walking very slowly, Elena carefully continued toward the road, hoping they wouldn't spot her. If they did, she'd have to explain why she was leaving so suddenly and with no warning. How could she tell them she was too afraid to stay? That whoever killed Jackson might kill her, too, if they found out she'd been listening at the door?

That wasn't the only reason, though, not by a long shot. Not only had Elena discovered Jackson may have been killed, but also that the man she'd fallen in love with had been lying to her. How could she have been so foolish? So careless? She'd always been so particular about whom she let into her heart; it was a habit she'd formed after being separated from her family at a young age and then having to live amongst strangers. Falling in love, though, wasn't something she'd planned. It just happened, and she couldn't have stopped it if she'd tried.

As a small, silent tear trickled down her cheek, Elena made it to the other side of the lodge without being seen. Breathing a sigh of relief, she picked up her pace and hurried on toward the road. Just before rounding the bend, she looked back at Black Wolf Lodge and sighed, wondering where she would go now. It wasn't easy, going to a new place and trying to fit in as someone of Hispanic heritage who spoke with a heavy accent. Mr. and Mrs. Levine had been so kind to her that she hated to leave, but they were gone now and it just couldn't be helped.

As Elena walked down the heavily wooded mountain road, she suddenly thought she heard the sound of footsteps. Turning, she peered back in the direction of the lodge, but the night was too dark to see anything. She stood in the middle of the road for a moment, listening and watching for any sign of movement, but the only sound that met her ears was the chirping of crickets. With a feeling of unease, Elena hurried on her way, wishing she'd thought to bring along a flashlight.

Just then, the loud snap of a breaking twig split the night air, and the hair on Elena's neck stood on end. Someone, or something, was following her, and she had no way of protecting herself. Holding the handle of her suitcase in a firm grip, she gathered her skirt in her other hand and began running. Did she hear the pounding of pursuing footsteps coming from behind? Or was that simply the pounding of her own feet? She couldn't tell, but when the howling of a wolf sounded in the distance, her breath caught and she had a distinct feeling that danger was close by.

As she ran, Elena tripped a couple of times on the rough and bumpy mountain road, and the steep downslope quickly caused her to go faster than she'd intended. Her chest heaving from fear and exertion, she knew that if she didn't stop herself soon, she was going to fall.

At the exact moment she skidded to a halt, a small car rounded the bend ahead of her, and Elena was bathed in its headlights. She raised a trembling hand to shield her eyes and quickly stepped to the side of the road. Her breathing was heavy as she turned to look back and see if anyone really was following her. Squinting as the car's lights illuminated the area, Elena thought she spotted a shadow slip behind the trees just up the road. Whether it was the shadow of a human or an animal, she couldn't tell, but all she wanted was to get down the mountain and to the safety of the bus station.

The car pulled to a stop beside her, and the window slowly rolled down as a familiar voice called out. Elena hesitated and glanced back up the road once again, still shaken over everything that had happened. Dare she get into the car? She had no choice. She had to leave this place, and she didn't wish to continue walking down this dark mountain road alone.

With a sigh, she headed toward the car, her hand outstretched to open the passenger door. As she climbed inside, she hoped she wouldn't regret the decisions of this night.

CHAPTER 1

Misty, *your mother was already pregnant when Karson met her. I'm sorry, but my son was not your father.*"

It had been two months since the woman Misty Raven thought was her paternal grandmother had spoken those words to her. Two long months and Misty had spent every single day since then trying to avoid thinking about them.

After discovering that Karson Himmel really wasn't her father, Misty was blindsided, to say the least. She'd gotten her hopes up once again, only to hit another dead end. She'd come back home feeling angry and exhausted and just emotionally burned out. So, for the last two months, she'd pushed thoughts of her parentage away and thrown herself into the house renovations. She refused to talk about or even think about who her birth father was, and since she'd asked those closest to her not to say anything, hardly anyone in town even knew what had happened. The last thing she needed right now was the good people of Shady Pines asking a lot of questions she couldn't answer.

It was a foggy morning in early April, and after fixing herself a cup of coffee, Misty got started on the renovations. They were coming along quite nicely, and Misty was hoping to be finished by the end of the year. After giving it some thought, she'd decided to turn the old place back into a B&B. She knew that would require a lot of extra work and planning, and although she didn't need the money, she wanted to settle down with a steady job. After selling Mr. Sikes' home, the man who'd been more like a grandfather to her than a neighbor, she'd invested the money and watched it grow into a very hefty nest egg. She was thankful for the security that money brought her and had always wondered what she would have done if it hadn't been for dear Mr. Sikes. She was so grateful for more reasons than one that he'd come into her life all those years ago.

Misty hadn't been working in her house for very long when her cell phone began to ring, and she quickly climbed from her ladder to see who the caller was. The name and number that flashed across the screen were listed as unknown, and when Misty tried to answer, the connection was muffled. The only clear thing she could hear was someone speaking her name, and Misty walked around the room, hoping to find a better signal.

"I'm afraid I can't hear you," she said as the line continued to crack. "Who is this?"

The voice on the other end sounded excited and also a little distressed, and when Misty thought she heard her mother's name mentioned, her heart quickened. Before she could figure out what was being said or who was on the other end of the line, however, the call was suddenly disconnected.

With a heavy sigh, Misty waited for a bit, hoping the person would call her back. When her phone simply remained silent, she attempted to get back to work, but all she could think about was that mysterious phone call. The connection was so muffled that she hadn't been able to identify the voice, and she felt frustrated that she may never know the meaning behind it all.

Finally, she decided to take a break from work and go for a walk with her St. Bernard mix, Wally. A thick blanket of fog lingered heavily in the air as the two stepped outside, and when Misty threw a stick for Wally to fetch, she quickly lost sight of his massive, furry body in the white mist.

They hadn't been outside for long when Wally suddenly barked, and the sound of a car coming down the driveway met Misty's ears. Wondering who would be visiting her house so early in the day, Misty called Wally to her side and held him by the collar. Peering into the fog, she could see headlights piercing the dense haze, but couldn't recognize the car just yet. Just then, the mysterious phone call she'd received came to mind, and she began to feel uneasy. Who would have been calling from an unknown number and mentioning Elena's name? Could the call have been some sort of threat?

Tightening her hold on Wally's collar, Misty spun around to go back into the safety of the house. Wally, however, held his ground as he continued to stare at the approaching car, his tail down. Before Misty could command him to come with her, a familiar voice suddenly called out.

"Buenos dias, Vega!"

Breathing a sigh of relief, Misty relaxed and waved to the driver of the car, which she now recognized as it emerged from the fog. Her old nanny, Mrs. Sanchez, had apparently come for a visit, and Misty was delighted to see her.

"Mrs. Sanchez, what a nice surprise," Misty said as Mrs. Sanchez climbed from the car. "Please, come inside. Would you like something to drink?"

"No, *estimada,*" she replied as Misty ushered her into the living room. "I tried to call you earlier, but my home phone has quit working, so I thought I'd just come over instead."

So, it was Mrs. Sanchez on the other end of the line earlier; Misty felt silly now for getting so upset about it. She then noticed that Mrs. Sanchez held an envelope in her hand, and when Misty sat next to her on the sofa, she held the envelope out for Misty to take. Her black eyes were piercing and filled with trepidation and a bit of…was it guilt?...as she studied Misty.

"I have a confession to make," she said, her Spanish accent thicker than normal. "I was going through some old boxes I'd put away in my attic years ago when I came across this picture."

Her brow furrowing in confusion, Misty opened the envelope and pulled out the old photograph, her eyes widening when she realized it was of her mother. Elena was sitting on a porch swing with a little girl…Misty…sitting on her lap. The two were both looking at the camera and smiling, and Misty's heart leaped within her chest. Other than the tiny, blurry picture in her locket, this was the only other photograph she'd seen of her mother. My, how beautiful she was! She looked so happy, and her sparkling black eyes were filled with obvious warmth and love for her daughter. Misty's own eyes filled with tears, and she looked up at Mrs. Sanchez questioningly.

"On my birthday, your mother gave me that photograph as a gift," Mrs. Sanchez explained, her voice a bit choked with emotion. "She knew how much I loved you and would adore a picture of you, but you would rarely smile for the camera unless she was holding you. After the two of you disappeared and I never knew what happened, I put the picture away because it was too painful for me to see. As the years passed, I forgot all about it. I'd like you to have it, Misty."

Pressing the picture to her heart, Misty smiled softly at Mrs. Sanchez and said, "Thank you so very much. You have no idea what this means to me."

Nodding, Mrs. Sanchez took a deep breath and said, "That's not all. If you look closely at the picture, you'll notice your mother was wearing a

North Georgia College t-shirt."

Surprised, Misty looked at the photo again and realized that Mrs. Sanchez was right. "But I thought you said she went to college in Atlanta?" Misty asked.

Mrs. Sanchez nodded, sighing heavily. "That's the confession I needed to make; I had your mother confused with one of my other clients. When I saw that picture, I suddenly remembered that Elena went to college in Dahlonega, *not* Atlanta."

Misty sat in silence for a moment, letting this new information sink in. She'd attempted to call a few of the colleges in Atlanta, but no one would even consider giving out information to someone who couldn't prove they were a relative. Would Dahlonega be any different? Probably not…and even if they were, would the college even have records dating back that far?

"I also remembered something else."

At Mrs. Sanchez's statement, Misty shook herself from her thoughts and looked at her old nanny hopefully.

Pushing away a stray piece of gray-black hair that had fallen across her forehead, Mrs. Sanchez said, "I remember your mother telling me she worked at a lodge in Dahlonega during her senior year of college. When I asked her why she left, she wouldn't say much at first, but later told me about a young man named Jackson who was killed under mysterious circumstances." Mrs. Sanchez paused and rubbed her temple as she tried to remember everything Elena told her. After a moment, she continued, "I can't recall everything she said, but Elena was afraid to stay in Dahlonega after that. I got the feeling she thought he was murdered, and that she *knew* the murderer."

Misty was taken aback by this news. There was so much about her mother that she didn't know, and would quite possibly never know, but after doing the math in her head, she realized her mother would have left Dahlonega around the time she became pregnant. Could Misty's father possibly be from that area?

"Do you happen to remember the name of the lodge?" Misty asked hopefully.

Mrs. Sanchez nodded. "Yes. It was Black Wolf Lodge."

That night, as Misty was getting ready for bed, her thoughts were filled with the conversation she'd had with Mrs. Sanchez. After her old nanny left, Misty immediately began researching Black Wolf Lodge and was shocked to find that it was still open. She'd called the lodge and spoken to one of the owners, Frankie Martel. Mrs. Martel stated that she remembered Elena working there, but that was the extent of the information she obviously was willing to give. She hadn't been very nice or forthcoming, and Misty ended the call feeling both hopeful and frustrated all at the same time.

Her cellphone vibrated just then, and Misty was a little surprised to see Adam Dawson's name flash across the screen. Shortly after their kiss in January, he had to go out of town on a job, and Misty didn't see him for almost a month. When he returned, she'd just gotten the news that Karson Himmel wasn't her father and she wasn't in the frame of mind to start dating. She asked if they could just be friends for a while until she could process everything, and at first, Adam was very understanding about it. As time passed, however, and Misty continued to keep to herself, he gradually stopped texting and calling and she hadn't heard from him in almost three weeks.

"Hey there, stranger. How are the renovations going?"

Misty stared down at the message for a moment, trying to gauge her feelings. In one way, she'd missed Adam, and it was nice to hear from him again. In another way, she still wasn't sure she was ready to date yet. Maybe he was okay with that, though. Maybe he was just reaching out as a friend.

"I don't think I realized what an undertaking this house would be when I bought it," she replied. *"But I've been able to make a lot of progress the last two months. How are you doing?"*

"I'm good. I left yesterday for North Carolina; I landed a big contract and will be working here for a few weeks. Maybe when I get back, we can get lunch…I've had you on my mind lately."

Misty didn't immediately respond; she wasn't sure what to say. She'd always enjoyed spending time with Adam, but with everything that was happening, she wasn't feeling like herself right now.

Her phone vibrated again, and Misty read his second message, *"Just as friends *wink*."*

A smile pulling at her lips, Misty replied, *"Sounds good."*

She then told him about Mrs. Sanchez's visit, smiling when his reply was filled with excitement and encouragement.

"That's wonderful! Keep me updated if you find out more?"

"Will do," Misty responded. *"Be safe in N.C."*

After turning her phone on silent, Misty grabbed her laptop and settled into bed. She once again typed in the lodge's website, eyeing the large announcement that flashed across the screen. The lodge was celebrating its thirty-fifth anniversary and would be hosting a weekend full of fun and activities as a way to commemorate the event. What if she went? Would she be able to uncover anything, or was it a bad idea?

With a sigh, Misty closed the laptop and went to bed, but it took nearly an hour for her to fall asleep. All she could think about was her mother and Black Wolf Lodge.

CHAPTER 2

Misty, you *have* to go."

Misty and her best friend, Tori Barlow, were drinking coffee in Misty's kitchen the next morning. Misty had just told Tori everything, and just as she'd expected, Tori was overwhelmed with curiosity and excitement.

"I don't know, Tori," Misty replied, absently twirling a lock of her curly black hair. "Mrs. Martel didn't seem very interested in sharing information about Elena other than simply saying she remembered her. I've hit so many dead ends that I just don't know if I can handle another right now."

Tori reached over and squeezed her friend's hand. "You've been through a lot, and it makes sense that you're getting tired of trying. But, Misty, this is a major breakthrough! *This* may be what you've been looking for all these years." When Misty opened her mouth with more protest, Tori held up her hand and added, "Look, why don't I go with you? We'll have some girl time, and Mom can see about Wally. I hear Dahlonega is a beautiful place, and we'll just go have some fun while doing a bit of casual poking around in the process. It'll do you good to get away for a bit,

Misty. You've been stuck in this house for so long that we've all been worried about you."

Misty took a sip of coffee and quietly pondered her friend's words. She knew Tori was right; in her state of frustration, she'd pulled away from everyone that cared about her and slipped back into her shell of solitude and self-preservation. She'd needed time and space to sort everything out, but in the process, she'd quite possibly hurt those closest to her.

"I'm sorry I've been so distant lately," she said softly, her gray eyes staring down into the swirling black liquid which filled her coffee mug. "Not developing close relationships has sort of been my thing since…well, ever since I can remember. I often forget that I now have people who are willing to help carry my load."

With a warm smile, Tori said, "You have a *family* now, Misty, and families help each other through difficult times. Just try to remember that, okay?" Leaning back in her chair, she added with a playful shrug, "I haven't felt pushed aside, though, because I've literally forced you to talk to me at least twice a day."

Misty threw back her head and laughed. "That's true," she said, pulling her friend into a hug. "And I'm so glad you did. Tell your parents I promise to take them up on their offer to eat lunch with you all after church as soon as we get back from Dahlonega."

Her eyes brightening, Tori squealed and said,

"So, we're going?"

Misty smiled and nodded. "How about this Friday? I saw on their website they're celebrating thirty-five years of being in business and they are having a three-day weekend filled with fun and activities."

Tori clapped with excitement. "That's perfect! We'll have a blast, and they'll be so distracted by the festivities that they won't even notice all the questions we'll be asking."

After booking their two rooms on Misty's computer, Tori announced it was time she got to work.

"Everyone will wonder why I'm opening Shady Grinds so late this morning," she said, referring to her coffee shop.

As Tori washed her coffee mug and went to return it to the cupboard, she caught sight of a DNA kit pushed toward the back of the cabinet.

"Did you finally decide to try one of those DNA websites?" she asked, turning to look at Misty.

"Oh, I ordered that thing months ago," Misty replied, waving a hand in the air. "I've just never gotten the nerve to try it."

Tilting her head to one side, Tori asked, "Why?"

"I tried one a few years back, but it didn't give much information," Misty replied. "Plus, I never even knew my real name until recently, so what was I supposed to do? Send messages to everyone I matched with and ask if they lost a three-year-old with gray eyes twenty-five years ago?"

"True, but you could give this one a try now," Tori said. "It may offer better results."

After a moment of hesitation, Misty nodded and said, "You're right. I'll give it a shot."

When Friday morning arrived, Misty was a bundle of nerves. She could only hope that this trip wouldn't be a fruitless one. What if she ran into more dead ends? Or worse yet, what if she found her father, but he wanted nothing to do with her?

Stop worrying, she told herself, taking a deep breath. ***This is going to be a fun trip, regardless of what you do or do not find out about your parentage.***

Misty had just finished loading her suitcase into the back of her car when her cell phone rang.

"You're fifteen minutes late," Misty answered jokingly.

"I have bad news," Tori stated in a heavy tone.

Misty's heart dropped. "What's wrong?"

"Mom was going to run the shop for me today, so I came in early this morning to get all the baking done," Tori replied. "Well, I was almost finished when I started smelling something weird coming from inside the oven, and then it suddenly just stopped working. Can you believe it?"

"Oh, no." Misty moaned. "Did you call the repairman?"

"I tried, but he's out of town," Tori replied with

a sigh. "So, I called someone in Savannah; he's supposed to call me back within the next hour or so."

"Oh, I see," Misty said, chewing on her bottom lip. "Do you want to just plan to leave tonight, then?"

Tori hesitated. "I don't think I can go, Misty," she finally said with a groan. "Who knows if this guy can even come? I may have to track down every repairman within a hundred miles. And if I *do* find someone, they may say the oven can't be fixed and then I'll really be in a mess…"

Seeing that her friend was clearly stressed out, Misty hurriedly suggested, "Look, why don't we just plan to go to Dahlonega next week, or whenever you get all of this straightened out?"

"We've already paid for the rooms, and the money is non-refundable," Tori stated, and Misty could picture her friend pressing a dramatic, flour-covered hand against the side of her face. "Oh, there's Brice; he's probably wondering why I haven't left yet. Now I've got to tell him I can't go…wait a minute, I just had a brilliant idea!"

Misty raised her eyebrows and sighed, not even trying to keep up with her friend as she rattled on. She could hear Tori saying something to Brice, but couldn't tell what was being said.

"Okay, it's all set," Tori said, bringing the phone back to her ear. "Brice is going with you."

Misty's eyes widened. "What? Tori, I don't think…"

"He has a friend who lives there that he's been wanting to visit," Tori interrupted, ignoring Misty's attempt to protest, "and since we've already paid for the extra room anyway, he said he'd love to go. He'll pick you up in about thirty minutes; he's got to run home and pack a few things."

Pursing her lips, Misty asked in a stern tone, "Tori, this isn't your way of trying to set us up again, is it?"

With a gasp that felt a little forced in Misty's opinion, Tori declared, "*No,* absolutely not. I just hate for you to go alone, and I know Brice will enjoy seeing his friend again. Y'all will have a great time! I'm just upset I can't go...and over the fact that I may have to spend no telling what to repair this stupid oven. Anyway, send me lots of pictures, okay?"

With a relenting sigh, Misty said, "Okay, fine. I'll miss you, and I hope you can find someone to fix the oven."

"Thanks. Me, too. I'll see about Wally while you're gone."

Misty hung up the phone and went back inside to wait for Brice to arrive. He was one of the first people she'd met in Shady Pines when she moved here, and they'd become fast friends. Tori kept trying to set them up, but after going through a bad breakup with a woman he'd been engaged to a few years ago, Brice wasn't ready for a relationship and Misty understood. Nothing had ever happened between them, except for an almost-kiss under the mistletoe last Christmas, which was interrupted. He and his grandfather, whom they all lovingly called Pops, ran the local hardware store in town, and they were two of the few people who knew about the situation with her father.

A large, furry head nudged Misty's knee just then, and she reached down to rub her dog's ears.

"Plans have changed, buddy," she told him. "Tori is going to see about you now."

When Wally whined and looked up at her with those sad puppy-dog eyes, Misty laughed and said, "Don't be like that. You love Tori, and I won't be gone long."

She leaned over and kissed his head, her heart tugging a bit as she thought that, even though she really wouldn't be gone long, she would miss him terribly. Wally had become her family, and the two shared a bond that only a few lucky pet owners would ever experience.

Hearing the sound of an approaching vehicle, Misty knew that Brice had arrived and went outside to meet him. Tori's blonde-haired and blue-eyed cousin climbed from his truck with an excited smile on his handsome face as he asked, "Ready to go on an adventure, Miss Raven?"

CHAPTER 3

The five-hour drive to Dahlonega went by surprisingly fast. Brice kept Misty laughing with his outrageous stories from childhood, and by the time they arrived, they were both starving.

"What a charming town," Misty commented as they drove around, looking for a place to eat.

"This was once the center of a huge gold rush," Brice stated. "Maybe we'll find some gold while we're here."

They met Brice's friend, Luke, at an Irish-style pub, where Misty got Shepherd's Pie and Brice ordered fish and chips. The food was delicious, and the people were friendly. Luke was also very charming; he and Brice had met in college and stayed in touch ever since. He was tall and slender, with thick, black hair and sparkling dark eyes.

"Black Wolf Lodge is a nice place," Luke told Misty. "It's pretty far up the mountain and the area is very peaceful. The owners mostly keep to themselves, but they're well known in town and people like them. Especially Merrick; he and his twin sister, Frankie, took over running the lodge after their parents retired."

"I spoke with Frankie on the phone earlier. I take it her brother is nicer?" Misty asked, snitching one of Brice's fries.

Luke nodded. "Frankie is a little…well, let's just say if she didn't have her brother and husband to help carry things, they probably wouldn't still have a business."

"Do you know anything about Jackson Dagon's death?" Misty asked, changing the subject. "I tried to look it up online, but all I could find was his obituary. I guess it happened too long ago for any information to be available online."

An odd look passed over Luke's face, and he asked, "What brought that up? Do you know his family or something?"

Misty shook her head. "No, I just heard he died around the time my mother left Dahlonega and that his death was suspicious."

"I heard my mother talk about it a time or two," Luke said. "Jackson and several of his friends went on a hiking trip after graduation, and his body was found at the bottom of Devil's Cliff. All of his friends said they were asleep and didn't know what happened, but everyone was a little suspicious about that story. The police never could prove foul play was the cause of his death, though, and the case was dropped."

Misty tilted her head to one side as she listened, her thoughts swirling. "Who were his friends?"

Tapping his chin thoughtfully, Luke spoke slowly as he tried to remember. "I know that

Merrick, Frankie, and Hudson were there; that was before Frankie and Hudson were married. Oh, yes, their cousin was there, too, but I don't know him because he left town shortly after and never came back. There was also one more person…a female, I think…but I can't remember who." Shrugging, he added, "If I remember, I'll let you know."

The server refilled their drinks then, interrupting the conversation, and Misty took another bite of the delicious Shepherd's Pie.

"Do you know the reason they named the lodge Black Wolf Lodge?" Brice asked his friend after the server left. "Misty and I were talking about it on the way up here."

Nodding, Luke leaned back in his chair, and by the sudden sparkle that came into his dark eyes, Misty knew he had a story to tell.

"Legend has it, there is a lone black wolf that lives up in the mountains," he told them. "It's been spotted off and on for hundreds of years. My grandfather, who was a full-blooded Cherokee, called it Ayohuhisdi."

"What does that mean?" Misty asked.

Luke leaned in closer and said in a low voice, "Death. Every time Ayo is seen, someone dies."

Misty blinked in surprise, a chill creeping up her spine.

Brice's brow lowered in disbelief, and he stated matter-of-factly, "One wolf can't live for hundreds of years."

Luke shrugged. "Maybe it's a ghost, or maybe

it's the original wolf's offspring. My grandfather told me that when the white man first came to this area, a group of Indians tried to fight them off. When one of the white men killed the chief's daughter while she was out gathering herbs, the medicine man went to his camp and built a large fire."

As Luke told the haunting tale, his eyes dark and almost frightfully intense, Misty noticed he pulled a beautiful, beaded necklace from inside his shirt. He absently rubbed his thumb over the beads and toyed with the gray feather which dangled from the end, and Misty wondered if it had once belonged to his grandfather.

"The fire grew bigger and bigger," Luke continued, "and the smoke billowed out like a giant cloud. Suddenly, from within the smoke, a black wolf emerged. It howled once and then leaped off into the forest, where it disappeared within the shadows of the trees. My grandfather said the white man who killed the chief's daughter was found the next day, mauled to death."

Shivering, Misty said, "What a creepy story. But why would anyone name their lodge after a death wolf?"

"Because it's become somewhat of a legend around here," Luke replied, "and legends tend to draw in the tourists."

"But saying that someone dies every time the wolf is spotted is a little over the top, don't you think?" Misty asked, raising an eyebrow.

Luke shrugged once again. "Maybe. But the night Jackson Dagon died, a black wolf was seen."

"I wonder if my mother knew anything about the wolf," Misty muttered softly to herself. Shaking her head, she sat up straighter and pointed to Luke's necklace. "What kind of necklace is that, Luke?"

Looking down at it in surprise, as if he'd forgotten it was there, Luke said, "Oh, this was my grandfather's. It's an original Native American necklace his father made for him."

"It's beautiful," Misty said.

The server appeared with their checks then, and the conversation about the wolf and necklace was over and forgotten. After paying for the meal, the three walked around town, with Luke playing tour guide. The history of the town was fascinating. They visited the gold museum, which is inside one of Georgia's oldest courthouse buildings, and Misty could just picture the mayor as he stood outside and declared, "There's gold in them thar hills!" She could sense the excitement that the people must have felt as they flocked to those very hills in search of a better life.

By the time they'd finished with their tour, it was getting late, and Misty and Brice told Luke they'd better head to the lodge.

"The cellphone reception is spotty up on the mountain," Luke told them. "So, make sure you're clear on your directions before you head up there."

"Are you going to be at any of the anniversary

festivities they have planned for this weekend?" Brice wanted to know, as he shook his friend's hand.

"I'll probably go to the bonfire tomorrow night," Luke replied with a smile.

As they began their trek up the mountain, Misty wrote the directions listed on her phone, just in case they really did lose reception. The road was narrow and winding, and with the setting of the sun and thick trees lining either side, it was getting difficult to see.

"I guess we should have left town sooner," Misty commented.

"Is this where I turn?" Brice asked, slowing his truck as they approached another road.

Glancing at her phone, Misty sighed when she realized Luke was right; there was hardly any reception. Checking the directions she'd written down, she nodded and said, "Yes, that's it."

Ten minutes later, a large wooden sign with "Black Wolf Lodge" engraved across the top came into view, and Brice turned down the long, gravel driveway. Shrouded in trees, the lodge could be seen just up ahead, and Misty felt her breath suddenly catch in her chest. This would have been the same drive her mother must have taken dozens of times. Was she happy while working here? Did she make many friends, or did she keep to herself like everywhere else? Misty yearned to know more about her, and when Brice parked before the large, cabin-like structure, she said a quick prayer under her breath to find more answers.

While Brice got their suitcases from the back, Misty stood still for a moment, taking it all in. Luke was right; it was very peaceful here. Crickets chirped, lightning bugs flashed randomly from the trees and bushes, and Misty could hear the trickling of a stream or brook nearby. The lodge was lit up with lights, while the rest of the property was covered in a blanket of darkness.

Suddenly, Misty heard a rustling in the woods to her right, and she shivered as a rush of cool air swept over her. Yes, it *was* peaceful, but also very remote and isolated.

"Ready to go in?"

Jumping slightly, Misty grabbed Brice's arm and laughed. "Yes, sorry. I guess I'm a little jumpy all of the sudden."

"Sure is a big place," Brice commented as they walked up the wooden steps leading to the veranda, which was decorated with string lights, several rocking chairs, and two swings on either side.

They walked through the front door and into the reception area, but there didn't seem to be anyone around. The décor was very rustic, with hand-carved furniture dotting the interior, paintings of landscapes and wildlife hanging on the walls, and folk pottery perched upon many of the surfaces.

"Where is everyone?" Misty wondered out loud.

"I don't know, but the place seems deserted." Wiggling his eyebrows mischievously, Brice added, "Maybe we'll have the whole place to ourselves."

Just then, a door behind the front desk opened, and a woman in her early fifties stepped out. She was tall and slender, with short, slicked-back dark hair and what appeared to be a pair of beautifully made beaded Native American earrings dangling from her ears. When she spotted Misty and Brice, her piercing blue eyes widened slightly.

"I didn't hear anyone arrive," she stated matter-of-factly. "Do you have reservations?"

Misty nodded. "Yes, we do," she replied, handing the woman a paper with her reservation number on it.

Without a word, the woman took the paper and pulled up Misty's reservations on the computer. Just then, the door behind the desk opened once again, and a man who appeared to be around the same age as the woman stepped out.

"I thought I heard voices out here," he said with a friendly smile. Extending his hand across the desk, he added, "I'm Hudson Martel. This lovely lady who is checking you in is my wife, Frankie. We are the owners here, along with Merrick, my brother-in-law. Have you stayed with us before?"

Misty and Brice shook his hand and introduced themselves. "I'm the one who called the other day asking if you remembered a lady named Elena who used to work here," Misty said to Frankie.

Frankie simply smiled tightly and nodded, while Hudson's eyes widened with delight. "Elena

Moreno?" he asked with a smile. "My goodness, I haven't thought about her in years. Do you know her?"

Misty's heart jumped, and she swallowed past the sudden lump in her throat. Her mother's maiden name was Moreno? Hudson Martel didn't know it, but he'd just placed yet another missing piece into the puzzle of Misty's past.

Before Misty could respond to Hudson's question, the front door swung open and a cold wind blew into the room. Shivering, Misty turned to see a man wearing a black coat step inside. He was of average height and weight and also appeared to be in his early fifties. His hair was thin and gray and he sported a small gray mustache, but it was his eyes that immediately caught Misty's attention. They were a light brown, but it wasn't necessarily the color; it was more of the cold, straightforward way in which they seemed to stare right through her. It set Misty on edge, and without thinking, she took a small step closer to Brice.

Suddenly, Misty heard a loud gasp from behind, and she quickly turned to see that Frankie's face had gone completely pale as she and Hudson stared at the man in shock.

"Terrence," she whispered in a hoarse voice.

"Frankie," the man replied in an almost cynical tone. "Aren't you and Hudson happy to see me?"

By the looks on their faces, Misty could tell they were definitely *not* happy to see him, and she was very curious to know why.

CHAPTER 4

Frankie visibly shook herself and cleared her throat. Pasting on a smile, she ignored the man as she handed Misty and Brice their room keys and said, "You're both upstairs, third and fourth rooms on the right."

"Uh, yes, and we're also serving supper out on the back deck until seven-thirty if you're hungry," Hudson added, forcing a smile of his own. "Please, let us know if you have any questions."

Nodding, Misty and Brice took their keys and headed up the stairs. As soon as they made it to the second floor, Misty stopped and listened to the conversation between the three below.

"This certainly is a surprise, Terrence," Hudson said with a slight, forced chuckle. "It's, uh, been a long time since we've seen you."

"Yes, almost thirty years now," Terrence replied.

Brice was halfway down the hall when he realized Misty wasn't with him. Turning, his brow furrowed in confusion when he saw her still standing at the top of the steps.

"What are you doing?" he asked.

Waving her hand, Misty held up a finger to shush him. She was convinced this was the cousin Luke had mentioned earlier, and she wanted to hear what they all had to say about this unexpected visit.

"What made you decide to come back?" Frankie asked, and Misty strained to hear his response.

"I'm currently going through a pretty nasty divorce," Terrence stated, "and when I saw online that y'all were having an anniversary celebration, I thought it would be a nice time to come back for a visit."

Tip-toeing back down the hall to stand next to Misty, Brice leaned over and whispered, "Why are you eavesdropping?"

"I'll tell you in a minute," Misty said, swatting his hand away when he began flicking her earlobe.

"Well, I'm afraid we don't have any available rooms for you to stay in…"

"Oh, I booked my room last week," Terrence interrupted in a triumphant tone. "I used the name Terry Teal; Teal was my mother's maiden name, you know. I thought it would be fun to surprise you all."

A door suddenly slammed from down below and Misty could hear footsteps walking toward the stairs. Annoyed by the interruption, she took Brice's arm and pulled him back down the hall where he'd left their suitcases.

"What was that all about?" He wanted to know as they unlocked their adjoining rooms.

"I think that man was the cousin Luke told us about," Misty replied in a low voice. "The one who disappeared after Jackson Dagon was killed."

A young woman appeared at the top of the stairs just then, and Misty smiled and nodded as she opened the door to her room and stepped inside.

"Why are you so interested in this Jackson fellow's death?"

Misty turned to see that Brice had followed her into her room, and she quickly walked over to shut the door so that no one could overhear their conversation. Tossing her room key on a nearby table, she opened her mouth to explain, but was quickly distracted as she looked around the room. "Wow, this is really nice," she commented.

"And there's even a balcony," Brice stated as he walked over to the double doors across from her bed and flung them open.

Misty joined him outside, the cool air sweeping through her curly black ponytail and tossing it over her shoulder. The night was dark, but Misty could tell there would be a glorious view of the mountains come morning.

Leaning against the balcony railing, Brice made certain to keep his voice down as he asked once again, "So, are you going to tell me what's going on inside that pretty little head of yours?"

"Mrs. Sanchez thought my mother may have known something about Jackson's death," Misty told him. "Apparently, she suspected that he may have been murdered."

Brice shook his head. "She must be where your nosy gene came from."

Slapping playfully at his arm, Misty laughed. "I am *not* nosy; just curious."

"Okay, whatever you say," Brice replied as he held up his hands in surrender. "Want to go back downstairs for supper?"

Misty nodded in agreement, and just as they turned to go back inside, she thought she heard the snapping of twigs from down below. Leaning over the balcony's railing, Misty looked down into the darkness but couldn't see anything. Suddenly, she had the eerie feeling that someone was down there in the darkness, listening to their conversation.

You're imagining things again, she told herself, rubbing her arms as a chill crept over her skin.

"Coming?"

At Brice's question, Misty nodded and hurried after him, thoughts of a shadowy eavesdropper drifting from her mind.

The back deck was lighted and full of people, and the heavenly smell of barbecue wafted through the air. Misty and Brice filled their plates and pushed their way through the crowd to find a table, smiling and nodding to everyone as they passed.

"A lot of the townspeople must be here," Misty commented when they sat down. "I don't think they have this many rooms here at the lodge."

"You are correct about that."

Turning in surprise, Misty realized the couple at

the table next to theirs overheard her comment.

With a smile, the woman said, "Most of the people here tonight aren't staying at the lodge. My husband and I, however, live nearly an hour away, so we'll be staying."

"Are you friends of the owners?" Misty politely asked.

"Yes, we've…well, *I've* known them my whole life," the woman replied, glancing at her husband. "My husband met them after we were married. I'm Evelyn Hall, by the way. This is my husband, Caleb."

Misty and Brice introduced themselves, stating that it was nice to meet them. The couple appeared to be in their early fifties, and Misty immediately noticed the expensive jewelry Evelyn was wearing. She was very pretty and petite, with shoulder-length blonde hair and sparkling green eyes. Caleb had a long, narrow face and balding head, with a kind, but rather shy smile.

"Where are y'all from?" Evelyn wanted to know.

"Shady Pines," Misty replied.

When they both asked where that was, Brice explained, "It's a little town outside of Savannah."

"Oh, I love Savannah," Evelyn stated with a sigh. "We rented one of those historic condos downtown last spring for a few weeks, and it was just gorgeous!"

"So, you were raised with the owners?" Misty asked Evelyn.

Evelyn nodded. "Yes, Frankie and I have been

best friends since grade school."

"Do you know Terrence, too?"

Evelyn blinked in surprise at that question, and Misty ignored the way Brice obscurely rolled his eyes.

"Frankie and Merrick's cousin?" Evelyn asked. "Yes, I know him, but how do *you?* He moved away years ago."

With a casual wave of her hand, Misty said, "Oh, I don't know him. Brice and I had just checked in when he arrived. I overheard him talking to Mr. and Mrs. Martel."

Evelyn's eyes widened. "You mean he's *here* now?"

Misty nodded, and Evelyn glanced over at her husband, who continued to sit quietly.

"My goodness, I wonder what made him come back after all these years," she said with a small laugh that seemed a bit forced. Clearing her throat, she added, "Well, it was very nice meeting the two of you. Caleb and I are due to join another couple in the game room in a few minutes. Caleb, honey, are you ready?"

Caleb nodded, and the two said their goodbyes as they hurried away, their heads together as they whispered to one another.

"Boy, you sure know what to say to get rid of people in a hurry, don't you?" Brice asked with a smirk as he sipped his sweet tea.

Leaning her elbows over on the table, Misty grinned mischievously and said, "Apparently not, since *you're* still around."

Brice laughed. "As hurt as I am by that comment, I have to admit that was a good comeback."

Just then, someone turned up the music that had softly been playing over the speakers, and couples began to dance. Standing up, Brice held out his hand and said, "Since you have been so hurtful, I feel that you at least owe me a dance."

Smiling, Misty took his hand and let him pull her into his arms.

"I'm not really dressed for dancing," she commented, pointing to her lightweight sweater and sneakers.

Brice shrugged his broad shoulders. "You look great to me," he replied, his eyes warm. Clearing his throat, he glanced away and asked casually, "So, does Adam know about this trip?"

"Yes," Misty replied, not bothering to expand on that subject any further. She'd told Adam over text message that she and *Tori* were going on the trip; she hadn't told him yet about Brice. Would Adam be angry or hurt about it? They didn't have any hold on each other, and she and Brice were just friends anyway. Why then was she so hesitant to tell him?

Through one of the back windows, Misty suddenly caught sight of Evelyn and Frankie, and thoughts of Adam were pushed to the back of her mind. The two women were standing in a corner by themselves, and by the looks on their faces, they were having a very intent conversation. Misty was pretty good at reading lips and thought she caught the words "Terrence" and "no good" in their conversation. Apparently, Terrence's arrival had sparked a lot of angst amongst his friends and family, and Misty's curiosity only grew stronger.

CHAPTER 5

That night, Misty's eyes drifted open and she blinked a few times in an attempt to clear the black film that seemed to rest upon them. Everything was so dark and quiet; where was she? She shivered and slowly sat up, moving her hand atop the blanket that covered her. Suddenly, it struck her, and she remembered she was at Black Wolf Lodge.

Shifting to her left, Misty felt along the edge of the bed until she found the lamp that rested on the bedside table. With a sharp *click,* a small glow lit the room and Misty glanced around, wondering what had awakened her. Just then, she realized the white noise on her phone had shut off, and with a sigh, she reached for her phone to turn it back on.

A sound from outside met her ears then, and Misty looked up, a shiver racing down her spine. It was unlike any sound she'd ever heard before, and she quickly climbed out of bed to go out onto the balcony. The moon was covered by clouds and the wind whispered through the tops of the trees, but Misty listened for the sound she'd heard only seconds before. A lonely sound, far away, but loud enough to echo through the mountains and intrude upon the depths of her sleep.

There it was again, and Misty felt her breath catch. She'd suspected as much, but couldn't be sure until she heard it again. It was the howling of a wolf, and as she listened, Misty knew it wasn't the cry of a pack, but from one lone wolf.

The next morning, Misty crawled sleepily out of bed and slipped into her robe with a yawn. After being awakened by the wolf's howls, she'd laid in bed with a million thoughts swirling in her mind. She didn't believe in ghosts and knew the story of the black wolf was just that: a story. But just the idea of hearing a wolf howling in the mountains after listening to Luke's story was enough to keep her awake for far too long.

Misty walked to the balcony doors and swung them open, her breath catching at the glorious view that awaited. The sun shone through the tops of the trees, its golden hues touching the mountains that stretched out as far as Misty could see. The air was cool, birds chirped happily among the treetops, and a soft layer of fog drifted peacefully along the mountain peaks. It felt as if she'd stepped into a painting, and Misty took a long, deep breath, soaking it all in.

Just then, a knock sounded on the door that adjoined Brice's room, interrupting her peaceful moment of solitude. With a sigh, Misty opened the door to find Brice fully dressed and apparently ready to take on the day.

"Good morning," he greeted her with a smile. "Ready to get breakfast?"

Cocking an eyebrow, Misty asked drolly, "Do I look like I'm ready?"

With a mischievous grin, Brice leaned against the door frame and said, "You look great to me."

Misty had to purse her lips to keep from smiling. "Give me a few minutes to shower and change, and I'll join you downstairs," she told him.

After taking a quick shower, Misty hurriedly slid into a sleeveless button-down khaki dress, white canvas sneakers, and a sweater. She pulled her curly mass of hair into a high messy bun, grabbed her purse, and hurried downstairs to find Brice.

Uncertain of where the breakfast room was, Misty went into the reception area to ask someone. There was a man standing at the front desk, his attention directed toward a stack of papers before him, and Misty paused a moment to study him. In his early fifties, he was tall and well-built, with black hair and a strong chin. His complexion was olive, and when he realized he wasn't alone in the room, he looked up and Misty was struck at how beautiful his smoky blue eyes were.

"You must be Merrick," she stated when he looked at her in surprise.

A pleasant smile broke upon his handsome face, and he nodded. "Yes, ma'am, that's correct. And you are?"

Misty walked to the desk and held out her hand.

"Misty Raven," she said. "I arrived last night."

"It's very nice to meet you, Miss Raven," he replied as he shook her hand. "You must have met my sister and brother-in-law last night."

Misty nodded. "Yes, I did. You and your sister are twins?"

Merrick's eyebrows raised in surprise. "Yes, we are. Is the resemblance that strong?"

"You *do* look a lot alike, but a local friend of ours told me," Misty replied. Taking advantage of the fact that no one else was around to interrupt, Misty cleared her throat and asked, "Do you happen to remember Elena Moreno?"

Merrick blinked. He opened his mouth to speak, but no sound came out at first. "Uh…yes," he finally said. "Yes, I remember Elena. Why do you ask?"

Taking a deep breath, Misty said, "She was my mother."

Merrick stared at Misty for a moment, and she wondered what was going through his mind. Shaking his head as if to clear it, Merrick glanced down at his desk and asked softly, "You said *was.* Does that mean Elena…?"

Misty nodded in response to the unasked question. "Yes, she passed away when I was only three."

With a look of sadness passing over his face, Merrick covered her hand with his and said in a gentle tone, "I am so sorry to hear that. She…she was a lovely woman."

"Thank you," Misty replied with a smile. "I'm sure you're busy right now, but if you get a chance, I'd love to talk more. I don't have many memories of her, so anything you could tell me would be greatly appreciated."

"Oh, I have a few minutes now," Merrick said, glancing at his watch. "Have you eaten yet? If not, why don't we talk over breakfast?"

Misty readily agreed and followed him through the reception area, down a short hall, and into a large room that smelled of freshly fried bacon, grits, hash browns, pancakes, and an array of other breakfast choices. The room was crowded, but Misty spotted Brice sitting at a table by the windows and pointed him out to Merrick.

After filling their plates, Misty and Merrick were heading across the room to join Brice when a woman who was standing at the beverage station caught Merrick's attention.

"Misty, this is our wonderful and beloved cook, Delta Coffey," Merrick introduced them. "Delta, this is Misty Raven, one of our guests."

"It's nice to meet you, honey," Delta said in a deep, throaty voice. Standing nearly six feet tall, she was a large-boned woman, with swarthy skin and gray hair cut short just above her shoulders. She had a wide, friendly smile, and wore glasses that framed large hazel eyes. She looked to be a few years older than Merrick, perhaps around fifty-eight or so, and Misty noticed that on her left ear only, she wore a Native American earring with a feather dangling from the bottom.

"Did you make the barbecue last night?" Misty asked.

"I had a little help, but did most of it myself," she replied, and Misty noticed how she kept busy while they talked. Delta struck her as someone who never sat still for very long.

"Well, if breakfast is half as delicious as the food last night, I know I'm in for a treat," Misty told her with a warm smile. "Are you from this area?"

"I sure am, sugar," Delta replied with a nod. "Born and raised."

Another guest approached Delta with a question about the vegetarian options, and Misty and Merrick excused themselves.

"Has Delta worked here long?" Misty asked after they'd taken their seats, and Merrick and Brice were introduced.

Tilting his head as he thought it over, Merrick said, "You know, I believe she started working here shortly after your mother disappeared."

Misty's eyes quickly darted from her plate of pancakes up to Merrick's face. "Disappeared?" She questioned.

Merrick nodded. "Yes, we never knew what happened to her. She worked here for a little over a year, and one morning when we got up to eat breakfast, she was gone. She left a small note with an apology for having to leave so suddenly, but that was the last we ever heard from her."

Misty mulled over Merrick's words for a

moment as she sipped on her cup of coffee. "Was…was she dating anyone?" she finally asked.

Merrick didn't answer for a moment; perhaps simply because he was in the middle of taking a bite of his scrambled eggs. Finally, he shrugged his shoulders and simply said, "Maybe, but I don't know for certain."

"Were the two of you friends?" Brice asked.

"Yes, as a matter of fact, we were quite good friends," Merrick replied. "We were in some of the same classes at the university. It took me a full year to get the courage to talk to her, and another year to actually develop a friendship." Chuckling, Merrick shook his head and added, "Your mother was quite the challenge; she kept to herself and made it very difficult for most people to approach her. I have always been a friendly type of person, though, so I guess I wasn't as daunted by the challenge as most."

Misty smiled softly at his words. She'd heard almost the same story from nearly everyone who'd known her mother. Why had she kept herself so distant from everyone? Was she simply very shy, or did she have a painful past that kept her from drawing too close to anyone? Perhaps she and Misty were more alike than Misty realized.

"How did she come to work here?" Misty asked.

Merrick took a sip of his orange juice before answering. "She worked in the university's library until one of the professors made a smart remark about someone who didn't speak perfect English working in a library. So, they transferred her across campus to work in the cafeteria. She stayed there for a year, and even though she never complained, I knew she hated it."

Misty's heart clenched. "Was she not treated well there?"

Merrick leaned back in his chair and sighed. "It was never anything super obvious; they'd just put more work on her than they would most of the other workers, and none of them were very nice to her. So, I finally convinced her to come work at the lodge, and she would ride to and from classes with me and Frankie."

Misty tilted her head curiously. "She and Frankie were friends, too?"

Merrick blinked. "Uh, well…"

Just then, Terrence Levine walked into the room. Merrick spotted him first, and Misty watched as his jaw clenched and his shoulders became tense. He didn't say anything, but Misty could tell he was no happier to see his cousin than his sister was.

Terrence surveyed the room with the casual air of someone who was very self-assured. His eyes landed on Evelyn and Caleb Hall, and with a smirk pulling at his lips, he walked to their table and sat right next to Evelyn. Misty watched as the woman glanced at him in surprise, then shifted away from him in her seat when he draped his arm around the back of her chair.

Clearing his throat, Merrick stood and said, "Excuse me."

Brice and Misty watched as Merrick walked over to Terrence. With the ease of someone used to handling tense situations, he patted his cousin's shoulder and asked if he could show him around the place.

"It's been a long time since you've been here, and I'd like to show you some of the updates we've done around the place," Merrick told him.

Terrence agreed, and with a flirtatious grin directed at Evelyn, he followed Merrick from the room. Evelyn said something to her husband, but Caleb only sat there quietly.

"That Terrence fellow sure is causing a stir," Brice commented. Leaning his elbows over on the table, he asked, "Are we exploring the grounds on our own today or participating in the events the lodge has planned?"

Grabbing the celebration brochure she'd picked up in the lobby the night before, Misty read over it and said, "At noon, the lodge is hosting an arts and crafts show, with tables and booths being run by local vendors. So, I'd say let's explore for a bit until then. Okay?"

"Sounds like a plan," he replied.

As Misty and Brice stood to leave the breakfast room, Misty noticed that Caleb finally said something to Evelyn, but she couldn't tell what. Just before they exited the room, she heard Evelyn say in a frustrated tone, "I've told you before; it never meant anything."

CHAPTER 6

Tori

It was nearly two o'clock, and the repairman still hadn't shown up. After finally returning her call the day before, he'd promised to be at her shop by noon on Saturday. As annoyed as she was, though, at least **he'd** returned her calls when no one else did. Apparently, getting someone to work on the weekend was nearly impossible.

The bell above her door jingled just then, and Tori was surprised to see her old science teacher, Patrick Donovan, walk inside. He'd lived with his wife, Sandra, in Shady Pines for as long as Tori could remember. After his wife's death, he'd retired from teaching and bought an old restaurant in town, which he'd renamed *Pat's Kitchen.* The restaurant usually kept him so busy that Tori rarely saw him during business hours, so she was pleased to see him now.

"Mr. Donovan, what a pleasant surprise," she greeted him. "How did you manage to get away from the restaurant?"

"I snuck away," he replied with a chuckle. "I had to hire a second chef last week, and listening to those two constantly bickering about how the food should be cooked is driving me crazy. So, I thought I'd take a break and visit one of my favorite old students. I've been craving a cup of your special coffee."

"Well, for my favorite old science teacher, you can have a cup on the house," she told him. "Plus a muffin. I don't have as much of a selection today, though; I had to make them at my house this morning since my oven here at the shop is messed up."

"You can use one of the ovens at my restaurant if you need to," Mr. Donovan told her. "Just let me know when you'll need it, and I'll make sure it's available for you."

Her heart warming at his thoughtfulness, Tori smiled gratefully and said, "That is so kind, Mr. Donovan. Thank you so much."

While Tori was pouring the coffee, her cell phone chimed, and she grabbed it up, hoping it was the repairman. It was from Misty instead, but Tori was still happy to hear from her friend.

"I would have called instead, but reception is too spotty," she texted. *"Is your oven fixed yet?"*

"Not yet, unfortunately," Tori stated out loud. When Mr. Donovan looked at her questioningly, she told him about Misty's text and how the repairman hadn't shown up yet.

"Is Miss Raven out of town?" Mr. Donovan asked as he took the muffin and cup of coffee from Tori.

Tori nodded. "Yes, she's in Dahlonega."

Raising his eyebrows in surprise, he asked,

"Why is she there?"

Tori hesitated. "Uh, she and I were supposed to go together for a girl's trip, but I had to back out due to this oven aggravation."

Another customer came in just then, and Tori was thankful for the interruption. She wasn't sure if Misty would want people to know the real reason she was in Dahlonega; the locals in town knew too much of her business already. But that's how it is when you live in a small town. As of now, however, only the Barlow family and Adam knew about Misty's situation with her father.

"Hey, Tori," the customer greeted her as Mr. Donovan waved goodbye and left.

Tori smiled at Noah Welch, who was one of her old classmates.

"Hey, Noah, how are you?"

As Noah began sharing all of his latest woes, Tori sighed inwardly. She'd always tried to be nice to him, but he was one of those people who was never happy and always had something terrible going on in his life.

"Well, since your cat is sick and you're having such a bad day, why don't I give you a muffin on the house?" Tori finally asked, interrupting him. At this rate, she wasn't going to make any profit at all today.

With a sigh, Noah nodded and said in a heavy tone, "That would be lovely, thank you."

After Noah left, a few more customers came and went, and Tori was just about to give up hope that her oven would be repaired when a large white truck parked on the curb in front of her shop. After grabbing a large tool chest from the back of the truck, a man wearing a navy blue and red uniform walked inside. He looked to be in his early forties, with shaggy brown hair and cool blue eyes.

"Miss Barlow?" he asked. When she nodded, he said, "I'm Julian Cooper, the oven repairman."

Tori breathed a sigh of relief. "Oh, thank goodness! I was afraid you'd forgotten me."

"Yes, well, I'm here now," he replied. His voice was very monotone, without feeling or emotion, and oddly enough, the expression in his eyes was exactly the same. "Where is the oven?"

Tori took him into the kitchen, and without a word of apology for being so late, Mr. Cooper immediately got to work. As there were no customers out front for the time being, Tori stayed in the kitchen as well and mixed up some batter for a coffee cake she planned to bake later in either her own oven or Mr. Donovan's. Julian Cooper did not try to make conversation, and after attempting to ask him a couple of typical, friendly questions, Tori finally gave up. Mr. Cooper's replies were short and clipped, and Tori had the feeling she was annoying him.

The next hour dragged by. After a while, Mr. Cooper went down to the hardware store for some parts, and Tori only hoped Pops would have them. When he returned, he didn't say a word; he simply got back to work.

It was nearly five o'clock when Mr. Cooper stepped into the main room and asked Tori to rejoin him in the kitchen. Her heart pounding, Tori hurried after him and anxiously waited for the news.

"Well, I was able to get it fixed," he stated, and Tori could have wept for joy.

"Oh, thank you so much, Mr. Cooper," Tori said with a relieved smile. "You have no idea how happy that makes me."

Nodding, Mr. Cooper said, "You're welcome," and then simply stood there for a moment, staring at her. They were all alone, and Tori shifted uncomfortably, wondering if he'd forgotten to say something else.

"Uh, how would you like payment?" she asked.

Waving a hand, he replied, "Our company will send you an invoice on Monday after I've turned in the ticket."

Tori nodded and opened her mouth to thank him again when he suddenly took a step toward her. Surprised, Tori immediately backed away, her shoulder connecting with a couple of hanging pots. They banged together loudly, and Mr. Cooper flinched, stopping in his tracks.

"I'll be going now." He cleared his throat and turned to gather his tools.

Just then, Tori heard the bell jingle over the door, alerting her to the arrival of a new customer. With a smile, she bid Mr. Cooper goodbye and hurried out into the front room.

"Good evening," a deep voice greeted her, and Tori looked up to see Officer Dylan Mitchell standing on the other side of the counter. He came in every afternoon just before Tori closed to buy whatever baked goods she had left over. He was in his early thirties and had moved to Shady Pines a few months ago after serving in the military. He had dirty blonde hair, brown eyes, and a strong jaw, and although Tori was curious to know what had brought him to Shady Pines, he was always very vague with his answers.

"Hi, Dylan," she greeted him. "I'm afraid my inventory is low today, but I have some peanut butter rice crispy treats left, along with a slice of cheesecake."

"I'll take it all," he replied.

Tori always wondered if he ate everything he bought from her shop himself or if he gave it to the men at the department, but she never asked. While she packaged up his order, Julian Cooper emerged from the kitchen and walked through the shop without a word. Moments later, she saw his truck pull away from the curb. He hadn't been the nicest fellow she'd ever met, but she was so thrilled to have her oven fixed that she didn't even mind.

After Dylan left, Tori closed the shop to do some baking in her newly repaired oven. Once she was finished, she locked up and headed to Misty's house to see about Wally. Ten minutes outside of town, she turned down the long, pine-shaded driveway that led to the beautiful, two-story

Victorian-style house. The sun was just beginning to set, but the woods were so thick around Misty's house that it almost seemed to be completely dark already.

As Tori walked inside the house, she smiled at the sound of Wally barking frantically from the kitchen.

"I'm sorry I'm not your mom, buddy," she said with a laugh as the massive dog jumped forward to sniff at her hands. "But I'm better than nothing, right?"

Tori let Wally out the back door to do his business and then proceeded to bang around the kitchen, looking for his dog food. She was so focused on what she was doing that she didn't hear the slight creak of the front door as it opened and closed. When she found the dog food, she poured a huge amount into Wally's bowl and also refilled his water supply.

Just then, the kitchen light went out and Tori froze, blinking her eyes rapidly as she tried to gain her bearings. There was no wind or rain, so what made the electricity go out? She was about to reach for the counter to feel her way to the light switch when the clicking of footsteps suddenly met her ears. They were slow and steady, and she immediately recognized the **whooshing** sound of the swinging kitchen door as it swung closed.

With her heart in her throat, Tori slowly turned around and squinted through the shadows cast by the shaded window above the sink. There, on the other side of the table, she could just barely make out the large silhouette of a man.

With a gasp, Tori jumped backward, her hip banging painfully against the counter. The silhouette stopped, but Tori could feel his eyes boring into her like the sharp edge of a spear.

"Wh-who are you?" She stammered, her voice shaking. "What do you want?"

Without answering, the shadow remained completely still for a split second, and the silence that hung heavily in the room screamed in Tori's ears. Then, before she could think of what to do, he lunged across the room toward her.

CHAPTER 7

With an ear-shattering scream, Tori took off toward the back door, her heart nearly pounding out of her chest. She grabbed the handle and tried to twist it open, but her hand was so sweaty that it slipped off. Before she could grab for the handle again, he was upon her.

His hands gripped her elbows, and he hurled her away from the door. She fell into the kitchen table, her thigh striking the solid mahogany as the chairs scattered across the floor with a loud screech. Ignoring the pain in her leg, Tori scrambled toward one of the chairs and hurled it at him just before he could grab her again.

With a grunt, he stumbled backward, and Tori took the chance given her. Forcing her trembling legs to propel her forward, she ran around the table and out the kitchen door into the living room. She stopped for a brief moment and blinked in the dimness, trying to gain her bearings. She could hear his footsteps coming from behind, and she took off in a blind rush, tripping over a piece of furniture as she went. Her arms flailing, she managed to catch herself and continued on toward the front of the house.

She heard the kitchen door open and knew he was only a couple of seconds behind. Her mind whirling, everything around her seemed to blend together into one shadowy blur. The furniture, walls, doors…it all swirled around and around like the funnel in a tornado. She could barely make sense of where she was going, but by some miracle, she found the front door and lunged toward it.

He was right behind her; she could almost feel him reaching out to grab her. With trembling fingers, Tori grasped the doorknob and twisted with all her might, feeling a brief second of relief when it turned easily in her hand. Throwing the door open, Tori rushed forward and slammed into the large body of a man standing on the other side.

Tori screamed and stumbled backward, fighting against the strong hands that grabbed her forearms. Through the haze of fear that blurred her mind, Tori somehow recognized the voice that spoke to her.

"Whoa, are you okay? What's going on?"

Tori stopped fighting and stared up at the man before her. She knew him…she would recognize those beautiful green eyes anywhere…but she couldn't make sense of what was happening. Spinning around, she saw the dark silhouette hurrying back through the house and into the kitchen.

"H-he's getting away," she stammered, pointing a shaky finger in the direction of the kitchen.

Her hero rushed into the house after him, while Tori stood frozen in place, her heart pounding so rapidly that she felt sick to her stomach. Just then, she heard Wally barking loudly, and she forced herself to follow the two men through the kitchen and out the back door. If anything happened to Wally, Misty would kill her.

As soon as Tori stumbled out onto the back porch, she heard the squealing of tires coming from around the side of the house. Wally was running at full speed through the yard in the direction of the retreating car, and Tori yelled at him to stop. Thankfully, he did, and she quickly called him to her side.

"Good boy," she said, tears filling her eyes as she leaned over and rubbed Wally's soft ears.

Just then, the sound of crunching leaves met Tori's ears, and she spun to see her savior walking around the house to join her on the porch.

"Tori," he said, his eyes widening. Apparently, he hadn't realized it was her until now. "What are you doing here? And what in the world just happened?"

Tori stared silently at her ex-boyfriend, Chris Caddel, still reeling with shock from everything that had happened. Chris had been her high school sweetheart for two wonderful years until he went off to college and suddenly ended things between them. Even though he still lived in the neighboring town of Cloud Haven, she hadn't seen him since the breakup and had never totally gotten over him. Seeing him again now, along with nearly being attacked by the intruder, was almost too much for her.

"I-I came to see about Wally," she stated softly, in a half-dazed state.

When she began swaying on her feet, Chris quickly grabbed her arm and led her inside the kitchen. After helping her into one of the chairs, he pulled out his cell phone and said, "I'm calling the police."

Tori sat at the table, trembling all over while Chris made the call. She kept expecting the man to leap out from behind the kitchen door or from inside the pantry, and she briskly rubbed her arms in an attempt to stop the chills.

"They'll be here in ten minutes," Chris told her after he disconnected the call. Hurrying to kneel at her side, he asked, "Do you want me to call your parents? I still have your dad's cellphone number."

Tori nodded. "Y-yes," she stammered, her teeth beginning to chatter. Was she going into shock?

The next few moments blurred together as Tori sat quietly at the kitchen table, not uttering a sound. Wally laid his head on her lap and whined as if he could sense the turmoil she was feeling. In all her life, she'd never been *attacked* before, and the thought of what could have happened if Chris hadn't shown up was almost unbearable.

"Hey, you're safe now," Chris said, gently taking her hand as he sat in the chair next to hers. "The police are going to catch this creep, okay? Don't worry."

In exactly twelve minutes, the sound of sirens met Tori's ears, and Officer Dylan Mitchell was once again in her presence.

"Who are you?" he immediately asked when he spotted Chris.

"Chris Caddel," he replied. "Miss Raven asked my grandfather to make a couple more rocking chairs for the front porch, but he couldn't remember the exact measurements of the first two. So, I stopped by to measure them when I heard a commotion coming from inside. I chased the guy around the side of the house, but he was already driving away by the time I made it there. He was driving a red Honda Civic, but that's all I could see."

Nodding, Dylan took down his name and number and then asked him to move aside. "Tell me what happened, Miss Barlow," he said, coming to sit next to Tori.

In jerky tones, Tori told him every horrible detail. Her parents arrived in the middle of the story, their faces filled with worry, and they stood supportively on either side of her as she finished.

"Do you know who it was?" Dylan wanted to know. "Did you recognize him?"

Tori hesitated and took a deep breath. Blowing it

out slowly, she raised her eyes to meet Dylan's and said, "I don't know for certain, because it was too dark. But…but I think it was Julian Cooper, the man who repaired my oven today."

CHAPTER 8

Misty

The area surrounding Black Wolf Lodge was beautiful and serene, but also very reclusive. Misty and Brice walked one of the trails before returning to the lodge for the festival, and it felt as if they were a million miles away from the rest of the world. The woods were dark and dense, but the trail they chose was peaceful, with a little brook bubbling and gurgling beside them. Birds chirped from the treetops, and they spotted quite a bit of wildlife as they walked.

By the time they arrived back at the lodge, the festival was well underway. There were at least sixty booths set up in the large, open area behind the lodge, with vendors selling anything from local honey to Native American jewelry. A local band played bluegrass music, and Delta Coffey stood behind a large wooden table serving a delicious array of refreshments. Much to Misty's surprise, the area was packed with people. Apparently, the locals didn't mind driving up the mountain for a bit of fun.

Misty and Brice strolled along the booths, each buying gifts for Brice's family. Misty also bought a bracelet for Wally's veterinarian, Kyra Kirby, and a plaid beret for Patrick Donovan. Both had become very good friends during her time spent in Shady Pines, and she was excited to give them their gifts.

"Do you want something to drink?" Brice asked, nodding his head toward Delta's table. "We've got at least fifteen more booths to go, and I'm thirsty."

Misty readily agreed, and the two stopped at the table to ask Delta for some lemonade.

"Here you go, honey," Delta said as she handed Misty her cup. "What made you two decide to come all the way up here from Savannah?"

Misty and Brice glanced at each other in surprise; how did Delta know where they were from?

"We're actually from Shady Pines," Brice corrected her with one of his charming smiles. "But Savannah is only about thirty minutes away."

Taking the opportunity while it presented itself, Misty said, "The main reason I came is because my mother, Elena Moreno, used to work here. Did you know her?"

Delta shook her head. "I believe I saw her around town a few times, but that was it. I was already finished with college when my sister, your mother, and the others around here were going."

"Your sister might remember her then?" Misty asked in a hopeful tone.

A flash of pain appeared in Delta's hazel eyes then, and she glanced away, blinking back tears. "My sister died during her senior year of college."

Misty's heart caught. "I'm so sorry," she said. "My mother passed away when I was only three."

"They were both too young to die," Delta said, shaking her head sadly. She looked over Misty's shoulder and nodded her head toward someone. "She actually dated Terrence Levine for a while before…before she died."

Misty turned to see Terrence standing at one of the booths only a few feet away. He must have heard his name mentioned because he turned and looked right at Misty and Delta. With a cool smile, he nodded to them and then continued with his shopping.

"Your sister dated him?" Misty asked, turning back to Delta.

Delta nodded. "Yes," she replied shortly. Looking at Brice, she asked, "Would you like more lemonade, sugar? Looks like you've already drained your cup."

While Delta refilled Brice's lemonade, Misty asked, "Terrence was with the group the night Jackson Dagon died, right?"

"He certainly was," Delta replied. Placing a hand on her hip, she said, "Now *that* was some strange goings on."

"What exactly happened?" Brice asked, leaning against the table as he sipped on the cool, sweet drink. "We've heard bits and pieces, but not the whole story."

Glancing around, as if to make certain no one was listening, Delta leaned over the table and said,

"The six of them went on a camping trip up in the mountains after graduation; they were a tight-knit group back in those days."

"Jackson, Terrence, Merrick, Frankie, Evelyn, and…?" Misty questioned, ticking off each name as she went. "Who was the sixth one?"

"Hudson," Delta replied. "He and Frankie had just started dating. From what I've gathered, Terrence and Jackson both had a thing for Evelyn, and they got into a fight over her on the trip. The next morning, Jackson was found dead. The police ruled it an accidental death; they said he must have been unable to sleep that night and went for a walk. They were camped out not far from a very tall and dangerous cliff, and Jackson must have gotten turned around during his walk and fell."

"None of the others heard anything?" Misty asked.

Delta pursed her lips and shrugged. "That's what they all said, but I have my doubts. I personally think that Terrence killed him, especially since he disappeared not long afterward and has only just now returned home."

Another couple approached the refreshment table then, therefore ending the conversation. Thanking Delta once again for the lemonade, Misty and Brice walked away. When they stopped at the first booth to do a bit more browsing, movement from the corner of her eye caught Misty's attention and she glanced in that direction. Her eyes fell upon Frankie, who'd apparently been standing on the back porch the entire time Misty and Brice were talking to Delta. The porch wasn't far from the refreshment table; had she overheard their conversation?

"It looks like you've found a lot of nice things," a voice to Misty's left stated, and she turned to find Evelyn standing beside her. Dressed to the T in a designer coat and carrying a Louis Vuitton purse, she looked almost ready to meet the queen.

"Yes, I have," Misty replied with a pleasant smile. "This certainly is fun, isn't it?"

Evelyn nodded, her blue eyes sparkling. "Yes, I'm having such a good time!"

Glancing around, Misty asked, "Where is your husband?"

"Oh, he's around here somewhere," she replied, shrugging. "He's probably over with the band, listening to the music."

"The music sure is great," Brice spoke up. "That banjo player is something else."

"Would you believe it if I told you I used to play the mandolin?" Evelyn asked, turning to face Brice.

While the two talked about music, Misty excused herself, stating that she'd like to take her packages up to her room before doing any more shopping.

"I'll wait out here for you," Brice told her.

As Misty walked across the grass toward the lodge, she bumped into Merrick and Hudson.

"Do you need help with those?" Merrick asked,

nodding toward her handful of bags.

"No, thank you," Misty told him. "I'm taking them to my room now. The festival is great, by the way. Brice and I are having a wonderful time."

Both men smiled with pleasure and thanked her, and when she walked onto the back porch, she nodded to Frankie and asked how she was doing.

"I'm fine, thanks," was her short reply.

Luke certainly was right, Misty thought. ***If not for Merrick and Hudson, this lodge would never have made it on Frankie's charming personality.***

As soon as she entered the lodge, Misty was struck by how quiet it was. Not a soul seemed to be around; all the employees and guests were apparently outside, enjoying the festivities. She quickly headed upstairs, her footsteps on the wooden staircase echoing through the lodge and bouncing off the walls to create a hollow sound within the lonely, empty building. Just before she reached the second floor, she heard a door open downstairs and assumed it must be Delta coming in for more refreshments.

With a sigh, Misty unloaded her packages onto the bed, hoping Brice would have enough room in his truck to take it all home. She then went into the bathroom to touch up her hair. As she searched for some bobby pins, she suddenly heard a loud creak out in the hallway. Pausing, she turned her head and listened for a moment. There it was again. It sounded like someone was outside her bedroom door.

Misty walked back out into her room, her brow lowering as she stood silently and waited. Perhaps one of the other guests was simply going to their room, but why hadn't she heard footsteps or a door closing? Instead, it seemed that someone was creeping quietly down the hall and had stepped on a creaky board.

Suddenly, the knob on her bedroom door began to jiggle, and Misty's heart jumped. Had she locked it? She couldn't remember. Why would someone be coming into her room without knocking first? She opened her mouth to call out for help but stopped. Who would hear her over all the noise outside? Hands trembling, Misty glanced frantically around the room, looking for a weapon.

With a squeak, the door started to open very slowly, and Misty backed away, her heart pounding. The hallway was dark and she couldn't make out any discernable features from the other side of the door, but she had the feeling that whoever it was meant to do her harm.

Just then, the sound of footsteps bounding up the stairwell met her ears, and Brice's voice called out, "Misty? Are you up here?"

Her bedroom door slammed shut, and Misty heard footsteps rushing away in the opposite direction. Legs trembling, she hurried out into the hall to catch a glimpse of her intruder, but it was too late. They had already escaped down the back stairs.

"What's wrong?" Brice asked when he reached

Misty's side and saw the look on her face. He touched her elbow, his eyes full of concern.

"Did you see who was at my door just now?" Misty wanted to know.

Brice shook his head. "No, I didn't see anyone. Why? What happened?"

"Someone was just trying to come into my room uninvited," she told him, her voice a bit breathless. "They ran off when they heard you approaching."

"Why would anyone be coming into your room?" Brice asked with a frown.

"I don't know," Misty replied, rubbing her arms. "Maybe they don't like all the questions I've been asking about Jackson Dagon."

Brice wrapped a protective arm around Misty's shoulders, and as they headed back downstairs, he said, "If that's the case, stay close to me from now on, okay? I don't want anything to happen to you."

Misty readily agreed, warding off an eerie sense of foreboding as she thought of what might have just happened if Brice hadn't interrupted.

CHAPTER 9

As soon as the sun began its descent, the vendors started closing their booths while Merrick and Hudson set about building several large bonfires. Delta traded her lemonade and cookies for s'mores and hot chocolate, and a local guitarist took over for the bluegrass band. Lightning bugs blinked like little stars in the evening dusk, and a chilly breeze whispered through the trees.

"There you two are!"

Misty and Brice were seated on hay bales at one of the bonfires when a familiar voice spoke out. Turning, they spotted Luke walking toward them.

"I've been here for a while now and wondered where you two were," he stated as he joined them. "Having fun?"

They both nodded, and Misty said, "It's been a wonderful day. Did you get a chance to browse through any of the booths before they closed?"

"Oh, yeah," he replied, nodding. "I bought a sweet, elderly neighbor of mine a pair of earrings for her birthday."

Just then, the sound of raised voices met their ears, and they turned to find Terrence and Hudson in the middle of what appeared to be an argument.

Hudson was trying his best to quiet his wife's cousin but wasn't having much luck, and his cheeks were turning red with embarrassment.

"Look, if y'all don't want me here, just say so," Terrence stated sharply. Apparently, someone had said something to anger him, and Misty quickly glanced around. Evelyn and her husband were standing off to one side; Evelyn's eyes were wide, and Caleb had his arm wrapped protectively around her waist. Frankie was hurrying off in the opposite direction, her shoulders stiff and rigid, while Merrick pushed his way through the crowd toward the two men.

"No one said we don't want you here," Hudson told him, attempting to keep his voice low. "We just don't want any problems."

"I don't think *I'm* the problem, Hudson," Terrence spat out.

"Come on, Terrence, let's take this inside," Merrick said once he arrived on the scene. Taking his cousin's arm, he all but dragged him up the back porch steps and into the lodge.

"What was that all about?" Brice asked softly.

"I saw him saying something to Evelyn a few moments ago," Luke replied as he sipped his hot chocolate. "He kept leaning close and whispering in her ear, and she wasn't backing away. When her husband showed up, though, things seemed to get awkward pretty quickly."

Delta Coffey walked by then, offering s'mores from a tray, and after she'd left, Misty looked at

Luke and asked, "Do you know what happened to her sister? She told me she died, but I hated to ask what happened."

Tapping his chin thoughtfully, Luke said, "I remember my mom talking about one girl she grew up with committing suicide, and I'm fairly certain it was Delta's sister."

Misty's eyes widened. "Oh, how tragic. Do they know why she did it?"

Luke shrugged. "Mom said she'd recently gone through a bad breakup while at the same time dealing with the loss of their father. I think it was just too much for her to deal with."

"That's really sad," Misty said with a sigh, her heart going out to poor Delta.

Just then, Hudson came back outside and was walking in their direction. Seizing the opportunity to be nosy, Misty casually asked, "Is everything okay, Mr. Hudson?"

Stopping, Hudson looked at Misty in surprise before immediately putting on a smile as he waved his hand and said, "Oh, yes, everything is perfectly fine. Just one of those family squabbles everyone has."

"I understand," Misty replied, her eyes drifting down to the bracelet he was wearing on his left arm. It was made up of a variety of stones and beads of all different colors and was connected by a thinly braided piece of leather. In the center of the bracelet, where it hooked together, was a sterling silver button with an engraved picture of an eagle. Pointing it out, Misty commented on how unique the piece of jewelry was.

Holding up his wrist to look at the bracelet, Hudson stated proudly, "It came from our local heritage museum. It was given to me as a gift, and I wear it nearly every day."

"It's beautiful," Misty said. "Would you like to join us for a moment? I haven't had a chance to ask you about my mother."

Nodding, Hudson sat down and said, "Yes, my wife told me about that. I'm so sorry to hear Elena passed away; she was a wonderful woman."

"Were the two of you friends?" Misty asked.

"We shared a few of the same classes and I often made a point to sit by her." Hudson paused and smiled softly, his eyes sparkling. "She was so beautiful that I just couldn't help but try, you know? She was very quiet and withdrawn, but there was just something about her that made every guy in class want the chance to date her."

"And *did* she date any of them?" Misty wanted to know.

Hudson glanced down at his hands, hesitating. "I...don't really know for sure," he replied, clearing his throat. "I wish I could help you more."

Misty tilted her head, studying Hudson as he spoke. Was it just her imagination, or did he know something he wasn't telling her? He wouldn't quite meet her gaze, and his face seemed to be a bit flushed. Perhaps it was just from the fire...or perhaps it was something else.

Before Misty could ask the next question on the tip of her tongue, Luke spoke up. "Weren't you dating Frankie at the time?" he asked, eyeing Hudson curiously.

"Oh, no, Frankie and I didn't start dating until almost the end of senior year," Hudson quickly replied.

Frankie appeared then, and Hudson immediately stood to wrap an arm around his wife's waist. "Hey, you," he greeted her. "Want to dance? That guitarist is playing our song."

Frankie nodded, and the two disappeared into the crowd. Was Hudson looking for an excuse to get out of the conversation about Elena, or was Misty simply reading too much into it? She had the feeling that Frankie had no desire to discuss her mother, but Misty intended to speak with her about it before they left, whether Frankie liked it or not.

Luke spotted someone he knew then and excused himself, leaving Misty and Brice alone.

"I'm not getting much information, am I?" Misty asked Brice, sighing as she stared into the fire. "Maybe I shouldn't have come at such a busy time."

"Hey, don't get discouraged," Brice said, reaching over to take her hand. "We've still got tonight and tomorrow, and at least you've made contact with everyone here. Who knows, maybe they'll remember something after you leave and call you."

Misty shrugged, feeling a little disheartened.

"Maybe so."

As they sat there, still holding hands, Misty felt grateful for Brice's presence. For so many years, she'd searched for answers on her own that it was nice to have the support of a friend.

A very handsome friend, too. Misty couldn't help but notice how the fire reflected in Brice's blue eyes, or the way his hair fell softly over his forehead. The long-sleeve, blue button-up shirt he wore stretched across his broad back, and Misty suddenly had the urge to lean her head over and rest her cheek against his shoulder.

Shaking herself, Misty pulled her hand away and said, "Goodness, it's suddenly gotten a little warm out here, hasn't it?"

Glancing over at her, Brice didn't immediately reply. Instead, he studied her for a moment, his eyes boring into hers as if he could read her every thought. Finally, he smiled and said, "I hadn't noticed."

Clearing her throat, Misty forced her attention away from her companion and looked around, searching for a diversion. After a moment, she spotted Terrence and Luke standing to themselves in what appeared to be a very deep conversation. Her brow wrinkling in confusion, she pointed it out to Brice.

"Didn't Luke say he didn't know Terrence?" she asked him.

Brice turned to see what she was referring to and shrugged. "They're probably talking business or something. At least Terrence seems to have cooled off."

The conversation between them soon turned to Shady Pines and more casual topics, and Misty finally began to relax. Why had she suddenly felt so…so flustered in Brice's presence? Perhaps it was just the romantic atmosphere, with the warmth of the bonfire and all the beauty surrounding them. She wasn't entirely certain, nor did she care to take the time to figure it out right now. She had more important things to think about.

That night, after the bonfire was over and everyone had either gone home or to their rooms, Misty took a nice, long shower. Once she'd finished, she put on a comfortable pair of pajamas and settled down to read a book. It was nearly ten o'clock when she heard something out in the hallway, and giving in to her curiosity, she climbed out of bed and opened her bedroom door. There, just across the hall, stood Terrence. He seemed to be listening at the door across from her room, and Misty wondered whose room it was.

"Can I help you?" she asked him with a raised eyebrow.

Jumping in surprise, Terrence spun around to look at Misty, his eyes wide. Then, his jaw clenching with aggravation, he said smoothly, "No, you cannot. Now, why don't you go back to bed?"

Her temper bristling, Misty replied, "Or perhaps I should call downstairs and tell them someone is lurking out in the hallway, listening at closed doors?"

His eyes narrowing, Terrence took a step closer to Misty and stated, "You're the one who's been asking so many nosy questions. Why do some people feel the need to be such busybodies? It might be better for them in the long run if they minded their own business."

Her fingers clenched into a fist at the veiled threat, but before Misty could respond, the door across the hall opened, and out stepped Merrick. Blinking in surprise at the audience, he glanced uncertainly between Misty and Terrence and asked, "Is there anything I can do for the two of you?"

"I was going to ask you the same thing, but it seems you've already been taken care of," was Terrence's snide reply as he looked over Merrick's shoulder.

Confused, Misty looked in the direction Terrence's gaze was pointed. Her mouth dropped open slightly when she spotted Evelyn Hall standing behind Merrick, wearing a bathrobe. Her husband, Caleb, was nowhere to be seen.

Merrick's jaw clenched, and Misty could see he was trying to hold in his anger. "I was assisting Mrs. Hall ***and*** her husband with the hot water in their shower. The knob was jammed, and I fixed it. End of story."

With yet another irritating smirk, Terrence turned without a word and walked back to his own room. Misty watched him go, her dislike for the man growing stronger by the minute.

Merrick closed the Hall's bedroom door, and Misty turned back to look at him, her cheeks flushing with embarrassment.

"I wasn't eavesdropping, Mr. Merrick," she told him. "I heard something out in the hall, and when I checked to see what it was, I discovered Terrence listening at the Hall's door."

With a sigh, Merrick ran his fingers through his hair and said, "It's okay, Miss Raven. I didn't suspect you of eavesdropping."

Hesitating, Misty said softly, "It seems that Terrence's return home has caused a bit of an uproar."

"You could say that again," Merrick replied with a humorless laugh. Shaking his head, he added, "Terrence was always a troublemaker, and it seems he hasn't changed a bit."

After bidding her good night, Merrick went downstairs and Misty closed her bedroom door. As she put her book away and climbed into bed, she wondered why Terrence had been listening at the door. Was Merrick truly fixing the hot water? Just because Misty hadn't seen Caleb in the room didn't mean he wasn't really there. Right?

Shaking her head, Misty turned off the light and slid under the covers. Who knew what was going on around this place, but she needed to stay focused. Her main reason for coming here was to find out more about her parentage, and she couldn't afford to get distracted.

Just before Misty drifted off to sleep, she heard the lonely, haunting sound of a wolf's howl. This time, it was much closer.

CHAPTER 10

Tori

Once the police finished asking their questions, Tori gathered up Wally and his things and left Misty's house.

"Hey, let me know if there's anything I can do, okay?" Chris told her before she left, his eyes filled with concern.

Instead of going to her own house, Tori went to her parent's home; she was just too shaken up to be by herself. They stopped at her house first for an overnight bag, and by the time they made it to her childhood home, she was exhausted.

"Are you going to call Misty and tell her what happened?" Neil Barlow asked as he helped bring the bag and Wally's things inside from the car.

"Not until she gets back," Tori replied with a shake of her head. "I don't want her to come home early on my account."

Her parents hovered over her for a while; they didn't say much, but she could see the look of worry written plainly on their faces. Dylan said they would be on the lookout for Julian Cooper, but what if they couldn't find him? What if he came back to finish what he'd started? Tori could hardly believe she'd spent so much time with the man at her shop that afternoon. Why hadn't he tried something then? Why had he taken the time to change vehicles and then follow her all the way to Misty's house? Perhaps the man who attacked her wasn't Julian Cooper at all. Could she have been mistaken?

By the time Tori went to bed, her head was pounding from all the unanswered questions that kept rolling through her mind. At least they were a bit of a distraction, though. When she wasn't asking herself questions, she was reliving every horrible detail of the attack, and that was even worse.

Wally roamed around the room for a bit before finally settling down next to the bed. Tori knew he was looking for Misty and felt confused about everything that was going on, but she was grateful for his comforting presence. Perhaps knowing a one-hundred-and-fifty-pound giant of a dog was laying guard beside her would help her sleep peacefully.

When Tori awoke the next morning, she was surprised to find a message from Chris awaiting her. He'd kept her number after all these years?

"How are you this morning?" He wrote.

Tori hesitated, wondering what her response should be. How **was** she, exactly? She'd barely gotten any sleep; every time her eyes closed, she'd seen the man lunging out at her from the shadows and could feel his hands gripping her arms. She couldn't stop thinking about it and wondered if she'd ever feel safe again.

"I'm okay," she replied. *"I didn't get a chance to tell you this yesterday but thank you so much for coming to my rescue. If you hadn't been there, I don't know what I would have done."*

Tori hit send, and with a sigh, pushed herself out of bed and went into the bathroom to wash her face. The events of the last eighteen hours were overwhelming; who would have thought some creep would attack her and then her ex-boyfriend would appear out of nowhere to save her? She hadn't seen Chris in so long that it felt strange to suddenly be back in contact with him.

Her phone alerted her to a new message, and Tori looked down to read Chris's response.

"You're very welcome," he texted. *"I'm just glad I was there. Keep me updated on the police search for this Julian guy, okay?"*

Tori said she would and then went downstairs for breakfast. Her parents were both up, and her mom already had homemade buttermilk pancakes on the table.

"Did you get any sleep, honey?" Amy asked, her worried eyes following her daughter's every step.

"I slept a little," Tori replied, knowing her mom had probably slept even less.

"Do you feel up to going to church? If not, I'll

stay home with you.”

“I feel up to going,” Tori replied as she sat at the table.

After eating the delicious pancakes, Tori fed Wally, got dressed, and headed to church with her parents. She hoped no one had heard the news yet; she didn’t feel up to answering a lot of questions just now. Unfortunately, her wish wasn’t granted. At nearly the exact instant she stepped through the church’s double doors, she was bombarded by a swarm of people.

“Honey, are you okay?”

“I can’t imagine how terrified you must have been!”

“Let me know what I can do, sweet girl. You know we have your back!”

Living in a small, southern town has its advantages at times, but Tori never ceased to be amazed at how quickly news could travel. She didn’t mind, though, really. During moments of crisis, she knew she could count on the sweet ladies from church or the beauty parlor to readily offer their comfort and support. Tori could still remember the time her mom had shoulder surgery and nearly every one of their friends brought cookies, pies, and casseroles to the house. Shady Pines was more than just a town; it was a family.

“I’m okay,” Tori assured everyone. “I’m sure the police will have him behind bars in no time.”

As Tori followed her parents into the sanctuary to take their seats, she discreetly covered a yawn.

She felt utterly exhausted but was still glad she'd come. Although she didn't quite feel up to dealing with all the attention and questions so soon, she realized it was better than sitting at home with a million thoughts running through her mind.

"Tori, I heard what happened. How are you?"

Looking up from her seat, Tori saw her old science partner from high school, Penny Atkins, standing at the end of their pew. Her boyfriend, Theo, stood next to her, not saying a word, but the way he stared silently at Tori always made her feel a little uncomfortable. Tori and Penny had never been very close, so she didn't know where Penny and Theo met. Someone said he lived in Savannah and they'd met online, but Tori had never asked Penny.

"I'm okay," she replied with a small smile. "Thank you for asking, Penny."

After the couple moved on, Patrick Donovan stopped by her seat. "The whole town has been in an uproar all morning about this," he told her. "Please let me know if you need anything, okay?"

Tori promised she would. She was thankful to have so many people who cared about her, but every time someone touched her on the shoulder, she would flinch in fear that it was *him.* Why hadn't Dylan called her with an update? Surely, they'd found him by now.

"Well, at least he fixed your oven," her father said later that afternoon as she pulled a loaf of banana bread from the oven. They'd stopped by after lunch to make certain Tori wouldn't have to be on the search for another repairman.

Tori nodded in agreement. "Yes, I'm glad about that." Hesitating, she asked, "Do…do you think I was wrong about him? Could it possibly have been someone else who attacked me?"

Neil shrugged and said, "I don't know, honey."

Her cell phone rang just then, and when Tori saw Dylan Mitchell's name flashing on the screen, she immediately answered.

"Miss Barlow, I have some news," he announced as soon as she answered.

Tori swallowed past the lump in her throat. "Yes?" she asked, her heart pounding as she put the call on speakerphone.

"I've been in contact with the Savannah police, and it seems that Julian Cooper is wanted in three other states for a long list of things," he stated, his voice heavy. "One of which is aggravated assault. They're trying to locate him, but it looks like he hasn't been back to his apartment yet."

Tori sat down and took a deep breath. "So, do you think he's left the area and I won't have to worry about him coming back?"

Dylan paused, and Tori looked up at her parents. She could feel their unease just as well as her own.

"I don't want to alarm you, but I don't think you should let down your guard just yet," Dylan finally said. "One of the women he assaulted in Florida said he stalked her for weeks before finally breaking into her home. I believe we'll catch him,

Miss Barlow, but until then, please be careful."

CHAPTER 11

Misty

The windows were rattling and a mournful, howling sound whistled through the mountains. Misty opened her eyes and looked at the clock; it was nearly eight in the morning. Throwing back the covers, she slid into her robe and went to the balcony. As soon as she stepped outside, she could feel something in the air; a heaviness, a sort of frantic urgency floating in the wind. The sun was hidden beneath drab, gray clouds, and when Misty leaned out and looked to her right, she could see the other guests packing up their vehicles.

A knock sounded on the door that adjoined Brice's room, and she hurried to let him in.

"Good morning," she greeted him. "I was just out on the balcony; it looks like everyone is leaving."

Brice nodded. "Yeah, I was just downstairs," he said, following her back out onto the balcony. "Apparently, there's a bad storm system heading this way. They're saying it's supposed to get pretty bad later this afternoon."

"Should we head home?" Misty asked, her

stomach clenching at the thought. She wasn't ready to leave; she had yet to get all the answers she'd come here seeking.

Brice shook his head. "No, it's coming from that direction, so we'd only end up getting caught in it," he replied, leaning his elbows over onto the railing. "Maybe it won't be as bad as they're predicting."

Brice went back downstairs, and after getting dressed, Misty joined him in the breakfast room. Evelyn and Caleb were there, as well, and Misty stopped to ask if they would soon be leaving.

"No, we're staying until Tuesday," Evelyn told her. "Now that we live in Asheville, I hardly get to see Frankie anymore, and the two of us have plans to do some shopping tomorrow in town."

"Well, hopefully, this storm won't be too bad," Misty said.

Terrence walked into the room then, and Misty fought back a sigh. It seemed he would be staying, too; she'd hoped he would leave along with the others. His presence here was causing too much of a disruption.

"It's normally not as bad as they predict," Caleb spoke up, and Misty glanced at him in surprise. He was normally so quiet that she'd almost forgotten he could speak. His gaze was focused on Terrence, however, instead of Misty, and she didn't miss the glint of dislike in his eyes.

"I hope you're right," Misty said, excusing herself. She went to the buffet, and as she filled her plate with Delta's deliciously fluffy biscuits and sausage gravy, she tried to keep her distance from Terrence. When he stepped toward her, though, and reached across her for the silverware, she clenched her jaw in irritation.

"Not going home today?" he asked, his breath only inches from her ear.

Stepping away, Misty shot him a glare and said, "No, we're not. Are you?"

Terrence shook his head and said, "Some would be happy if I did, but no. I'll be staying for a bit longer."

Misty tilted her head, studying him for a moment as he grabbed a napkin. "I heard you haven't been home in years. What made you come back now?"

Terrence looked at her in surprise. "What is it with you and your nosy questions?" He snapped. "What brought *you* here?"

"I'm searching for answers about my mother, Elena Moreno."

Terrence's eyebrows shot up. "Elena Moreno? Now that's a name I haven't thought of in years, but she's not someone I'd ever forget." Winking at Misty, he added, "No man ever could."

There was something about this man that made her skin crawl, but Misty forced herself to remain polite. "She died when I was three, and I'm trying to locate my father."

Her response surprised Terrence; Misty could see it on his face. After a brief hesitation, however, a spark formed in his eyes. Looking nonchalantly down at his fingernails, he asked, "Have you, uh, spoken to Merrick or Hudson about it? They might can help you."

Nodding, she said, "Yes, I've spoken to them both about it, but they don't seem to know very much. Do *you* happen to know anything?"

"Oh, I know a lot of things, but I don't think my dear, wonderful family would appreciate my spreading rumors," Terrence replied smoothly. "Unless you're willing to pay for what I know?"

The lewd, Cheshire cat grin that spread across Terrence's face as he looked her up and down made Misty want to slap him.

"No, thanks," she replied stiffly. "I'd rather not owe you anything."

As Misty spun on her heel and walked away, she could hear Terrence chuckling behind her.

Later that afternoon, Misty and Brice decided to go for a walk before it started to rain. When they stepped outside, they were surprised to see Luke pulling up.

"Mrs. Frankie called this morning and asked me to stop by and look at her computer," he told them as he climbed from his truck. "She said it wouldn't turn on this morning."

Luke was a computer engineer, and according to Brice, he was a genius when it came to computers. He owned a repair shop in town and also worked part-time at the college. Misty was surprised that he apparently also made house calls.

Glancing up at the sky, Luke added, "Looks like I'd better hurry if I don't want to get stuck up here."

Brice slapped him on the back and said, "We'll stop by the shop tomorrow morning on our way out to say goodbye. It's been really good to see you, buddy."

As Misty and Brice headed down one of the trails, Misty asked, "Does Luke's family still live in this area?"

"Luke never knew his father," Brice replied, "and his mother passed away from cancer right before we graduated from college. He's got a sister who lives out of state somewhere, and a few of his dad's relatives live up on one of the mountains. They're strange folks, though; I don't think Luke is very close to them."

"He mentioned his grandfather was full-blooded Cherokee. Was that his mom's father?"

Brice nodded. "Yeah, I met him a few times. He was unlike anyone I've ever known."

"How so?" Misty wanted to know.

Brice considered her question for a moment, his expression thoughtful. "He was very wise and told the most fascinating stories," he said, kicking a small rock with the toe of his boot. "Half the time, I wasn't sure if they were really true or fantasy. He always knew what the weather would bring, and could tell how deep a river ran just by looking at it. He was also an outstanding hunter and tracker. Luke told me when he was a young man, a bear killed his younger sister. He tracked that bear all the way across the mountain, and when he finally found it, he killed it with a knife."

"Wow, he sounds more like a legend than a real man," Misty replied.

Brice nodded, chuckling. "Sometimes a man can be both."

They were so engrossed in their conversation that neither Brice nor Misty was paying attention to how far they'd gotten from the lodge or how dark and foreboding the clouds had become. The wind was getting stronger and scattering leaves across the trail, and when thunder suddenly rumbled in the distance, they realized they'd better turn back.

The return walk to the lodge felt different as they hurried to beat the rain. Misty always got a sense of unease when a storm was in the air, and she felt it now as the sky steadily grew darker and a brisk wind lifted her hair and whipped it around her face. No wildlife could be seen, except for a few birds hurriedly flying to their nests. Tree branches overhead creaked and groaned, while the thick bushes that lined the trail rustled and shook. When the lodge finally came into view, Misty breathed a sigh of relief and quickened her steps.

Once inside, Brice went in search of a snack and Misty went upstairs to touch up her hair. The moment she entered her room, she stopped dead in her tracks. Something was different, only she couldn't quite put her finger on what it was. She walked slowly around the room, her eyes taking in every detail. Her bed was made and her suitcase was still lying open on the luggage rack, but her neatly folded pajamas and underclothes looked as if they'd been rummaged through. She went into the bathroom, noticing that her hairbrush and perfume weren't sitting exactly where she'd left them. Had someone been in her room? She'd left the "Do Not Disturb" sign out, so why would anyone have come in and gone through her things?

Shaking her head, Misty decided that she must be nervous about the storm and simply imagining things. There was no reason for anyone to enter her room and go through her things, and she quickly put the idea from her mind.

After touching up her hair, Misty grabbed a sweater from the closet and glanced out through the open balcony doors as she passed. Pausing, she took a closer look and realized the thick layer of fog that hung over the mountains was actually rain, and it was heading right toward the lodge. Thick, dark clouds billowed angrily overhead, and Misty knew the storm wasn't far off.

CHAPTER 12

It took nearly an hour for the rain to reach the lodge, but once it did, it beat against the building with fury.

"I'm going to jump in the shower before the lightning gets too bad," Misty told Brice.

"Good idea," Brice replied as the two headed upstairs to their rooms. "I'll join you."

At Brice's words, Misty caught her foot on the top stair and stumbled. Brice quickly caught her arm, and when she looked up at him, his cheeks were flaming red.

"Uh, that's not…well, you know what I meant," he stammered.

Pulling her arm away, Misty cleared her throat and laughed awkwardly. "Yeah, I know what you meant. Thanks for catching me, by the way. A fall down the stairs isn't exactly what I had in mind for this trip. Meet you in the dining room in thirty minutes?"

They went their separate ways, and within a few moments, Misty was enjoying a steaming hot shower. She could hear the thunder drawing closer, and so she hurried as much as she could; getting struck by lightning wasn't what she had in mind for this trip either.

After her shower, Misty got dressed and decided to go downstairs a few minutes early. She still hadn't had a chance to talk to Frankie and hoped that now would be a good time.

She'd just stepped out into the hallway when she heard the sound of voices coming from down the hall. Turning, she saw Terrence and Evelyn stepping from inside his room. Terrence had his hand on Evelyn's arm, and by the look on her face, she wasn't happy.

"You have no proof, Terrence," she hissed at him, jerking her arm away. "Now why don't you just go back to where you came from?"

Misty stepped back into her room but left the door cracked enough to hear what was being said.

"I plan to stick around for a while," he stated in his typical, snide tone. "You will just have to get used to it."

Evelyn stomped away without another word, and Misty heard her go into her own room and slam the door. She shut her own door and decided to wait for Brice; the last thing she wanted right now was another run-in with Terrence.

Sitting in the rocking chair by her bed, Misty thought over what she'd just heard. Had Terrence come back to Dahlonega to harass Evelyn about something? But how could he have known she'd be staying at the lodge during his visit? Had they perhaps been in contact with each other? If so, why had Evelyn seemed so surprised when Terrence showed up?

Shaking her head, Misty sighed heavily. None of it made sense, but she had no business putting her nose in it…unless it had something to do with Jackson Dagon's death. Did Terrence think Evelyn killed Jackson? Is that what her mother had suspected as well?

Suddenly, a loud knock sounded on her door, and Misty jerked in surprise. Realizing she'd been so caught up in her thoughts that the time had gotten away from her, she grabbed her purse and joined Brice out in the hallway.

"I looked for you downstairs, but couldn't find you," he told her, his skin and clothes smelling of soap and cologne. "Did you decide not to come down for supper?"

"Me, decide not to eat? Surely, you jest," Misty replied teasingly. "No, I just got caught up in…some stuff."

She considered telling him about the conversation she'd overheard but quickly decided against it. He'd probably laugh and call her nosy again, and he'd be right. Why did she always seem to get involved in things that were none of her business?

Twenty minutes later, Misty and Brice were seated in the dining, watching out the windows as the sky grew darker and darker. The rain seemed to have set in for good, and flashes of lightning lit up the sky every few seconds.

"Well, it looks like I'm stuck here for the night," Luke stated with a sigh as he joined them at their table.

"You should have left before the rain hit," Brice told him.

Luke nodded, his black eyes staring out the window. "I know, but I was so caught up in fixing Mrs. Frankie's computer that I lost track of time."

"Couldn't it have waited until tomorrow?" Misty wanted to know as she took a bite of the delicious baked salmon Delta had prepared. "It is, after all, a Sunday."

Luke shot Misty a look and said, "It's her work computer, and she said she **had** to have it up and running by tomorrow. She can be very demanding, you know."

Brice cocked an eyebrow. "This is why you need a work phone so you can turn it off on the weekends."

"I agree," Luke replied with a chuckle.

A blast of thunder rattled the windows just then, followed by a brilliant flash of lightning. Misty shivered and pushed herself back against her chair. It seemed this storm was going to be just as fierce as they'd predicted.

"Is Frankie available to talk?" Misty asked Luke.

Luke nodded. "Yes, and now that her computer is fixed, she's in a much better mood than she was this morning."

Asking the two men to wish her luck, Misty pushed her chair back and headed to the front desk. Just before she rounded the corner, however, she heard Frankie talking to someone.

"His presence here is causing problems," she was saying in a low tone. "I know you don't care for him either or I wouldn't be telling you this, but I think we all wish he would just leave."

"Maybe he'll take the hint and go home soon."

The voice that responded belonged to Delta, and Misty wondered what they'd been saying before she arrived.

"If he doesn't, something will have to be done," Frankie stated.

Misty suddenly heard footsteps coming from the staircase, and as she didn't wish to be caught eavesdropping, she cleared her throat and stepped around the corner.

"Good evening," she greeted the two women. "Delta, the salmon you made tonight was quite possibly the best I've ever had."

Delta smiled broadly. "That's so sweet, love. Thank you." Glancing at Frankie, she said, "Well, I'd better get to those dishes. I'll see you two later."

After she'd left, Misty walked over to the desk and tapped her fingernails nervously against the polished wood.

"Is there something you needed?" Frankie asked, raising a thin, black eyebrow in Misty's direction.

Assuming that someone like Frankie would appreciate a more direct approach, Misty took a deep breath and said, "Mrs. Martel, you know I came here to find answers about my mother, but I haven't been able to learn much at all. I'm leaving tomorrow, and I'm desperate to know the truth so I'm just going to ask point blank: do you have any idea who my father is?"

Frankie blinked, obviously taken aback by Misty's bluntness. She hesitated, glancing down at the desk where she was absently twirling a pen in her hand. Misty waited, barely breathing, and wondered if perhaps Frankie would tell her the truth…*if,* that is, she knew the truth.

When Frankie finally looked back at Misty, her face was hard and set in stone as she said simply, yet firmly, "No, I do not know who your father is. I'm sorry."

Feeling frustrated but determined to give it all she had, Misty pressed, "Do you perhaps know of anyone she dated?"

With a look of irritation passing her face, Frankie pursed her lips and asked, "How would I have known that? Your mother and I weren't friends. In fact, your mother wasn't friends with anyone."

Not particularly caring for the tone in Frankie's voice, Misty stated, "Both your husband and your brother told me *they* were her friends."

Frankie's jaw clenched and something akin to anger flashed through her black eyes. "Well, if *men* were the only friends your mother had, then I guess it would be impossible to say *who* your father could be," she replied in a cold, hard tone.

Her temper flaring, Misty had to force herself not to say something she would regret. Apparently, Frankie hadn't liked her mother and was more than reluctant to talk about her, and there was no point in sinking down to her level by being rude.

With a stiff nod, Misty simply said, "Thank you for your *help.* I won't keep you from your work any longer," and walked off.

By the time she made it back to the dining room, Misty was seething. How dare Frankie insinuate such a thing about her mother! If Misty could have rung the woman's neck and gotten away with it, she would have.

"Any luck?" Brice asked when she got back to the table.

Misty shook her head. "No," she replied. "She said she and Elena weren't friends."

"Elena?" Luke asked, his eyes getting larger. "That was your mother's name?"

"Yes." Misty nodded. "Elena Moreno. She went to college in Dahlonega and worked here at the lodge."

Shaking his head in disbelief, Luke leaned back in his chair and slapped his thigh. "My mother used to talk about a woman named Elena," he told her, excitement in his voice. "There's an old trunk back home full of pictures of the two of them. Misty, our mothers were best friends."

CHAPTER 13

Misty could hardly believe her ears. After Frankie's nasty comments, she had to admit she'd been feeling pretty low. Now Luke was telling her that his mother was one of Elena's closest friends. What were the odds?

"Luke, are you sure?" she asked, leaning toward him.

Luke nodded eagerly. "Yes, and I believe they corresponded through letters until your mother finally quit writing. Mom always wondered what happened to her."

"Did they go to college together?" Brice asked.

"No, mom didn't go to college," he replied, a lock of coal-black hair falling across his forehead as he shook his head. "She and dad got married right out of high school and she helped him on the farm. I think they supplied the college cafeteria with fresh vegetables."

"My mom worked in the cafeteria before coming to work here," Misty told him, excitement making her eyes sparkle. "I'll bet that's how she met your mom."

"You're probably right," he agreed. "I believe they also made deliveries here, as well, so the two of them probably saw a lot of each other."

"I'd love to see those pictures you have at your house. Your mom didn't happen to keep any of the letters my mother wrote to her, did she?" Misty asked hopefully.

"I think I remembered seeing some old letters in her trunk," Luke replied. "When I get home, I'll look and let you know."

Merrick stepped into the dining room just then, and when he spotted Luke, he headed their way.

"It doesn't look like this storm is going to let up anytime soon," he said, "and it's too dangerous to be out on those roads right now. Why don't you just plan to stay here tonight? We have several available rooms, so you can have your pick."

Luke nodded gratefully. "Thanks, Merrick. I think I'll take you up on that offer."

Slapping Luke on the back, Merrick looked out the window and sighed. "It sure is getting rough out there. We haven't had a storm like this in years."

"The news report said there's a strong chance for tornadoes," Brice stated.

"Let's hope it doesn't come to that," Merrick replied worriedly.

Standing, Luke said, "Well, I'm going to head upstairs and pick out my room for the night. I'll see y'all later."

Merrick and Luke walked out together, and Misty looked at Brice and said, "Can you believe mine and Luke's moms were friends? This is wonderful!"

"It's a small world," Brice replied with a shake of his head.

Delta came over to their table then and asked if they wanted anything to drink. They requested some decaf coffee, and when she brought back two cups of the steaming hot liquid, Misty asked, "Do you always work so late, Mrs. Delta?"

"No, I just wasn't able to get to my cabin in this storm," she replied. "Guess I'll be sleeping here tonight."

After she walked off, Brice commented, "It's a good thing those other guests left to accommodate everyone else that's gotten stuck here tonight."

Misty nodded in agreement. Thinking about Luke again, she asked, "Didn't you say Luke never knew his father? What happened to him?"

"He died around the time Luke's mom got pregnant with him," Brice replied as he poured a heaping amount of creamer into his coffee. "I think it was a farming accident or something."

"How sad," Misty said, feeling sorry for Luke. She knew how it felt to never have the love of a parent. "Does Luke still have the farm?"

Brice shook his head. "No, his mom sold it shortly after Luke's dad died."

The two sat and talked for a while more, and after the coffee was gone, they decided to try to get some sleep.

"I hope this storm blows itself out soon," Misty commented as they headed upstairs. "I've never seen a storm last so long."

"I think it's supposed to be like this off and on all night," Brice said. Winking down at her, he added, "If you get scared, let me know and I'll come over."

Misty laughed and slapped his arm. "Behave, Mr. Barlow."

Brice grinned, his blue eyes twinkling. "I can't make any promises, Miss Raven, but I'll try."

Misty bid him good night and went into her room. As she got ready for bed, she could hear the wind and rain beating loudly against the windows. When she was little, she used to imagine that a huge giant with a mighty fist would emerge from the storm clouds like a funnel from a tornado to pound at the windows, demanding to be let inside. As she never had parents to comfort her, she would always jump into bed with a large stuffed animal and bury her head under the covers until the storm would pass.

Turning off the lights, Misty climbed into bed and slid beneath the handmade log cabin quilt. Thunder shook the house every few minutes as brilliant flashes of lightning lit up the room, casting shadows that seemed to move and sway along walls. The paintings, furniture, and light fixtures all seemed to come to life, giving Misty an odd sense of apprehension. After a bit, she reached for her sleep mask and slid it over her eyes, hoping to block out the light and get a bit of sleep.

Twenty minutes passed and Misty had just drifted off into a light sleep when something suddenly jarred her awake. Pulling up her mask, Misty sat up in bed and listened. Angry voices were coming from the hallway, and unable to resist the temptation to see what was going on, Misty climbed out of bed and grabbed her robe.

"Stay away from my wife."

The hissed words that came from Caleb Hall's mouth were a surprise to Misty as she peered through the crack in her bedroom door. She hadn't known he was capable of showing so much emotion, but by the look in his eyes as he glared at Terrence, she realized he was the type who simply had to be pushed.

"Maybe you should tell your wife to stay away from *me,*" Terrence replied, his eyes glinting as he sneered back at Caleb.

When Caleb took a step toward him, his hands clenched into tight fists, Misty held her breath. Should she call for help before someone got hurt, or just stay out of it?

Before Misty could decide, Caleb spun on his heel and stalked into his room, slamming the door behind him. Laughing loudly, Terrence turned and went to his own room, his shoulders held high as he sauntered away.

Sighing, Misty closed the door and decided to read for a bit. She grabbed a blanket and settled down in the rocking chair, the old murder mystery instantly grabbing her attention. The more she read, the more engrossed she became, and she soon realized that a dark, stormy night perhaps wasn't the best time to read such a spine-tingling novel. In her mind's eye, she could see the dark scene unfolding before her and feel the intensity of the characters in the story. Chills swept over her skin and she gripped the book tighter as a murderer quietly stalked his victim from the shadows, slowly inching closer and closer. Suddenly, at the exact moment he wrapped his hands around her throat, a mighty clap of thunder shook the lodge so viciously that Misty gasped and jerked back against the wooden chair, her heart pounding. One second later, the room was shrouded in total darkness.

Trembling, Misty sat in stunned silence for a moment. The hair on her arms stood on end as electricity from the lightning strike surged through the house. After a moment, she slowly stood and felt her way through the dark room. If she could find her phone, she planned to go downstairs and ask the owners for a flashlight or some candles.

When she found her phone, she realized with a moan that it hadn't been charging after all and was almost dead. She'd barely made it halfway across the room when it died and her only light source was cut off.

Heaving a sigh, Misty set the phone aside and reached out to feel her way across the room. She'd just made it to the door when it suddenly opened and a light shined into her eyes. Shielding her face, she was unable to see who it was and quickly took a step back. A large hand reached out to grip her by the forearm, and with a startled gasp, she jerked away.

"Misty? Are you alright?"

Misty immediately relaxed when she recognized Brice's voice. "Yes, I'm fine," she said, sighing. "I don't think I've ever seen such a violent storm."

"I know what you mean…"

Before Brice could finish the sentence, a loud scream suddenly echoed through the house.

"Fire!"

CHAPTER 14

Misty and Brice rushed out into the dark hallway, the sound of pounding footsteps coming up the stairs nearly as loud as the storm outside. Light beams bounced along the walls as three figures emerged from around the corner, all carrying flashlights. Merrick was in the lead, his face tight with worry, while Frankie and Hudson crowded in behind him with pensive expressions. All the guests were peeking their heads out of their rooms as murmurs of confusion rippled down the hallway.

"What's going on?" Merrick asked, his voice tight with worry. "Did I hear someone say there's a fire?"

Suddenly, the door beside him was flung open, and Delta cried, "Mr. Merrick, there's a fire in the attic. Hurry!"

With a collective gasp, everyone immediately rushed past Delta and up the narrow staircase that led to the attic. Misty smelled the smoke before she saw the flames, and as soon as she reached the top of the stairs, her eyes widened in horror. The massive upper floor was alight with flames that were quickly spreading through piles of old decorations and dusty furniture.

Misty stood frozen in place as the heat from the flames swept over her skin and burned her eyes. Merrick quickly jumped into action and grabbed an old rug, while the other men pulled out moth-eaten clothes and raggedy blankets to start beating out the flames. Terrence stood back for a moment, looking on with an expression of annoyance as if he didn't care to get his expensive clothes dirty.

Shaking herself, Misty began to help Evelyn and Frankie pull as much stuff out of the way as possible, hoping the sparks wouldn't jump across the space and ignite the objects of their efforts.

"Here, honey, let me help you," Delta said as she jumped in to assist Misty with a particularly heavy trunk.

Suddenly, the men yelled and there was a loud crash. Choking on the smoke, Misty spun around, her heart pounding as she searched for Brice. When she couldn't find him, she felt tears of panic burning her eyes. Had something fallen on him? What if he was hurt badly, or trapped beneath the flames? Just as she was about to leap forward and start searching for him, she spotted him through the smoke and breathed a sigh of relief.

"Misty, help me with this!" Evelyn cried, and Misty quickly got back to work, her hands trembling as adrenaline rushed through her veins.

It seemed that time moved in slow motion and at the speed of light all at once. Misty couldn't get a coherent thought in her mind except to stop the fire before they all burned to death. The smoke was thick and burning her throat, and she felt trickles of sweat dripping from her forehead. Her hands were chaffed and stinging as she continued to shove roughened pieces of furniture out of the way, and she could hear the men grunting from behind her. Finally, after what seemed like hours, the fire was out and all that remained of the terrifying ordeal was smoke, ash, and a few dying embers.

"Men, can you help me carry up some buckets of water from one of the bathrooms downstairs?" Merrick asked, his voice filled with exhaustion. "I want to soak some blankets and towels and lay them around."

As the men went downstairs for the water, Misty and the other three ladies slowly looked around at the mess.

"It's a good thing you realized there was a fire, Mrs. Delta, or we all may have been trapped inside," Misty said as she brushed her hair away from her face.

"Yes, there's a cat that lives up here and I came to check on her after that horrible lightning strike," Delta said. "That's when I realized there was a fire."

Frankie glanced at Delta in surprise, and Misty had the feeling she hadn't known about the cat. She hoped Delta wouldn't get into any trouble because of it.

The men returned with buckets, blankets, and some extra flashlights for everyone. Misty noticed that Terrence wasn't among them; she assumed he thought himself above any type of manual labor and must have excused himself downstairs.

"Are you okay?" Brice asked Misty after they'd placed the wet blankets strategically about.

Misty nodded. "Yes, I'm okay. Are you?"

"Of course. I'm tough, remember?" He replied with a wink.

Misty's eyes filled with tears then and she said softly, "I thought for a minute there that…that you…"

"Yeah, that was a close one," Brice said, pulling her into a warm hug. "Everything is okay, though."

Misty rested her head on his chest and closed her eyes for a moment, listening to his heart beating against her ear. He could have been killed in that crash; she was so thankful he was alright.

"I tried to call the fire department, but the call won't go through," Merrick said as they all went downstairs. "One of the towers must be down. It looks like we're on our own until this storm completely blows over and someone can get out here."

"Let's hope it blows over soon," Evelyn stated.

As if to contradict her words, a clap of thunder reverberated throughout the house and everyone shivered.

"Merrick and Hudson will be keeping an eye on the attic all night," Frankie told everyone, her hair a mess and soot lining her forehead. "I'll be downstairs in our bedroom, though, so just let me know if any of you need anything.”

Everyone said good night, and as Brice took Misty’s hand and they headed back to their rooms, Misty suddenly felt exhausted. It had been a long weekend, and the stress of the fire just topped it all off. All she wanted to do was go to sleep.

“Oh, dear,” Misty muttered when they got to their rooms and she glanced down at her dirty pajamas. “I can’t go to bed like this.”

“Yeah, you look almost as bad as I do,” Brice said with a chuckle.

Misty took note of his appearance then, her eyes widening. His undershirt was torn and covered in soot and ash, and his pants had burn marks all over them. His blonde hair was a mess, and Misty gasped when she spotted blood trickling down his temple.

“Oh, Brice, you cut yourself,” she stated, reaching up to touch the wound gently. “I’ve got a small first aid kit in my purse. Come into my room and I’ll put some medicine and a bandage on that cut.”

“I think one of those beams must have bounced off my head when it fell,” Brice said as he lightly touched his temple.

After digging around for the kit, Misty instructed Brice to sit on the small sofa in her room and aim the flashlight at his head.

“I wonder how many people carry a first aid kit in their purse,” she said with a chuckle as she sat next to Brice. “I guess that must mean I get into trouble too often."

"Oh, you definitely get into a lot of trouble," Brice agreed, his gaze warm as he smiled at her.

As Misty leaned in close to tend Brice's cut, she found herself feeling a little too aware of his breath on her cheek. He smelled of ash and sweat and dust, but the underlying tone of his cologne that always made Misty think of the ocean still lingered beneath it all.

"You know, you're a sight in those polka-dotted pajamas, all covered in soot," Brice said, his voice low and filled with humor.

Misty chuckled and replied drolly, "I guess I shouldn't enter any beauty contests right now, huh?"

Reaching up to wipe a smudge of soot from her chin, Brice said softly, "Definitely not. It wouldn't be fair to the other girls."

Misty paused what she was doing and glanced at Brice uncertainly. They'd always had such an easy, playful friendship that she wasn't sure if he was serious or just teasing her. By the look in his eyes, though, she knew he was serious, and she suddenly felt warm all over. What she wasn't sure of, however, was if he was trying to flirt with her or simply being nice. He'd told her only a few months ago that he wasn't ready to have a relationship with anyone because of everything he'd gone through with his ex-fiancé. Could he have changed his mind, or was she simply reading too much into this?

When Brice touched her hand and his eyes slowly lowered down to her lips, a picture of Adam popped into Misty's mind and she jumped back, knocking the flashlight from Brice's hand.

"Whoa, did I burn you?" Brice asked, laughter in his voice.

Her cheeks flaming, Misty quickly stood and said nervously, "I, um, guess you did. Do…do you have any more cuts I need to see about?"

Brice picked up the flashlight and shook his head. "Nah, I'm okay," he said, standing to his full height to tower over her. He stood very close, and Misty swallowed past the sudden lump in her throat. "Thanks for seeing about my forehead."

Nodding, Misty slowly backed away and said, "You're welcome."

"I'll see you in the morning," Brice said before he left her room. "Let me know if you need me for anything, okay? It's been a rough night."

Misty promised she would, and then locked the door after he left. After washing off and changing her pajamas, Misty climbed into bed and snuggled up under the covers. She lay there for a while, thinking about the fire and Brice and what had happened…or almost happened…between them. Or was she simply imagining things? Perhaps Brice hadn't felt one thing and wondered why she'd jumped away from him like that. Her cheeks flushing, she flipped over onto her side with a huff, embarrassed for letting herself get so flustered.

Oh, stop overthinking and go to sleep, she told

herself.

Being able to force her mind to stop, however, was easier said than done. Misty lay in bed for over an hour, listening to the thunder rumble and the rain as it slapped against the side of the building. Finally, she got up and slipped into her robe to go downstairs in search of something to eat. The lodge always kept little packaged snacks in the eating area, and a cookie or cinnamon roll sounded nice right about now.

Misty pitter-pattered down the hall, her slippers swooshing against the hardwood floor as the flashlight beam bounced along the walls. Other than the sudden rumbles of thunder, the lodge was completely still and silent. It seemed that everyone was asleep, other than herself and whoever was keeping watch upstairs, and she heaved a sigh, wondering how the others were able to relax after such dramatic events.

The stairs creaked as Misty made her way from the second floor to the first. She tiptoed into the eating area and paused for a moment, blinking when a sudden flash of lightning lit the room. In the short moment of light, she could see out of the floor-to-ceiling windows that lined the walls of the dining room. Tree limbs swayed back and forth in the dark night like giant arms stretching out to grasp anything within their reach, while leaves and branches blew wildly about from the heavy wind and rain.

Suddenly, the lightning flashed again, and it

seemed that a black shadow emerged from behind the bushes. It stood at the window, staring inside, and Misty felt a cold chill race up her spine. When the lightning flashed again, it was gone, but Misty could have sworn that the shadow had belonged to a large black wolf.

When a loud blast of thunder shook the building once again, Misty was startled and grabbed the back of the nearest chair. She continued to stare out the window, carefully searching the darkness, but the shadow was gone. Had she really seen it?

Glancing toward the snack bar, Misty hesitated, not wishing to move from her position behind the chair. Something about the way the branches scratched at the windows and the wind howled through the hills brought every nerve of her body to the surface. Perhaps it was just the violence of the storm and the alarming events of the night, but Misty felt that something dark and sinister lurked within these walls. She hadn't felt it until now, and after seeing that shadow at the window, she was beginning to wonder if perhaps her imagination was getting the better of her.

Deciding to forego the snack, Misty turned and went back upstairs. She'd just made it to the second floor when she bumped her elbow on the corner of the wall and dropped her flashlight. Its light went out as it bounced and rolled down the hallway, and with a sigh, Misty bent over and felt along the floor.

Suddenly, she heard a loud thump from down the

hall, and she stopped to listen. The hallway was too dark to see, but Misty clearly heard the creak of a door as it slowly opened and someone stepped quietly from one of the rooms. Feeling disoriented in the darkness, Misty tilted her head, trying to figure out exactly where the footsteps were coming from as they headed in her direction. They were light, as if whomever it was didn't wish to alert anyone to their presence, and the same chill of foreboding that Misty felt before once again raised the hair on the back of her neck. There was no light and no sound in the blackened hallway; just the faint brushing of footsteps as they quietly came toward her.

"Who…who's there?" Misty whispered, her heart pounding.

At the sound of her voice, the footsteps stopped and Misty thought she heard a slight intake of breath. Feeling the desperate need to grapple around the darkness until she found the flashlight, Misty forced herself to remain still. She had the feeling that if she made any sudden moves, it might not end well for her.

Just then, the footsteps started up again, but this time they were much quicker and now heading toward the back stairs. Misty dropped to her knees and hurriedly felt along the floor until her fingers finally landed on the flashlight. Grasping it tightly in her hand, she quickly clicked it on and shined it down the hall, but she was too late. The person was gone.

Misty stood there for a moment, wondering what to do. She considered going down the hallway and knocking on the doors, just to make certain everyone was alright but changed her mind. After the events of the night, she didn't think anyone would appreciate being awakened out of a good sleep.

With a sigh, Misty went into her own room, firmly locked the door behind her, and slid back into her bed. As she drifted off to sleep, she listened as thunder rumbled loudly and the wind continued to howl through the mountains, and she wondered if this storm would ever pass.

CHAPTER 15

The next morning, the storm was finally over, but Misty could hardly believe her eyes when she walked out onto the balcony. Tree limbs, bushes, leaves, and various types of debris were scattered everywhere. Several trees had been snapped in half, and Misty could see shards of glass glistening in the morning sun.

"Wow," Brice breathed as he looked over her shoulder; he'd come into her room shortly after she'd finished dressing. "What a mess."

Misty shook her head sadly. "So much damage done to these beautiful surroundings."

After Misty grabbed a sweater, the two headed downstairs in the hope that some type of breakfast would be served. The electricity was still out, and Misty lightly rubbed her arms as she warded off a chill. However cool it was, though, she was glad it was April and not August. Summer in the south was brutal, especially without air conditioning. The weather in the mountains, though, seemed cooler than on the coast, a fact that Misty was thankful for at the moment.

When they arrived downstairs, an exhausted-looking Merrick sat behind the front desk, drinking a cup of coffee.

"Good morning," he said, covering a yawn. "Delta has breakfast cooking on the grill out back, so please help yourselves."

"Did you get any sleep?" Misty asked with a sympathetic smile.

Merrick shook his head. "No. I was too worried the fire would start back up again. I hope you did, though?"

"A little," Misty replied. Hesitating, she asked, "Since you were awake, did you happen to hear anything strange around two in the morning?"

Merrick thought it over for a moment before saying, "No, but I couldn't really hear anything up in the attic with the rain pounding on the roof. Did something happen?"

Misty shrugged and said, "I don't know. I heard a loud thud and then someone out in the hallway, but when I asked who it was, they didn't answer and ran down the back stairs."

Merrick frowned. "How strange," he said. "I'll ask around and make certain everyone is okay."

"Maybe someone was sleepwalking," Brice spoke up. "I used to do that when I was a kid."

Merrick said he'd ask around anyway, and with a nod, Misty followed Brice out to the back deck. Evelyn and Caleb were seated at one of the tables, both with a steaming cup of coffee and a bowl of cheese grits. The back deck had apparently been swept off already, but there was still quite a lot of debris left along the sides. Delta stood at the grill flipping pancakes on the griddle, and when she turned to greet them, Misty noticed how tired she looked.

"Did you get any sleep?" Misty asked her as she filled a mug with coffee.

"I sure did," she replied, although the swollen, dark circles under her hazel eyes spoke otherwise. "That ordeal with the fire wore me out; I slept like a baby afterward."

"When you get through with those pancakes, I'll take two," Brice told her, and Misty could almost see his mouth watering.

Just as they were sitting down with their coffee, Frankie and Hudson stepped outside.

"Do any of you need anything?" Hudson asked as Frankie helped herself to the steaming pot of cheese grits.

Everyone shook their heads, and the couple took a seat at the table next to Brice and Misty.

"Mrs. Martel, how long has your family owned the B&B?" Misty asked, attempting to be nice in spite of the woman's nasty comments about her mother the day before.

"Call me Frankie," she replied, and Misty was a bit surprised that the woman could actually be cordial. Her blue eyes drooped with exhaustion, and it seemed all the wind had gone out of her sails. "My grandfather first built this house in the 1940s for his family, but it was much smaller back then. After he and Grandma passed away when I was about fourteen, my parents decided to add a second floor and turn it into a lodge. Merrick and

I added the attic later. We have always loved the lodge, and I was very happy when Hudson wanted to help us run it."

Hudson smiled at his wife and reached out to pat her hand. "We've had a lot of good times, haven't we, honey?"

Frankie smiled tightly and nodded, but Misty didn't miss the way she slowly moved her hand out from under her husband's. Misty thought the reaction to be a bit strange, but with Frankie's personality, Misty assumed she simply wasn't big on outward displays of affection.

Merrick and Luke joined them shortly after, and once everyone had eaten and Delta started to clean up, Hudson suddenly looked around and asked, "Hey, where's Terrence?"

"Maybe he left during the night," Frankie muttered in a hopeful tone.

Elbowing his wife, Hudson said, "Perhaps I'd better go upstairs and check on him."

"You know how he is; he's probably just sleeping in," Delta stated with a slight harrumph.

Slapping his thighs, Merrick stood up and said, "I'll go with you, Hudson."

The two men went back inside, their heads together as they discussed something in low tones.

Glancing uncertainly at Frankie, Misty asked innocently, "Aren't you glad your cousin has come for a visit?"

Frankie shifted uncomfortably in her seat. "Terrence is just, well, Terrence," she replied in a dry tone. "He's about as welcome around here as a sore throat."

Before Misty could figure out a way to pry more, the patio door crashed open and Hudson stumbled out.

Spotting the stunned, ashen look on her husband's face, Frankie jumped to her feet and asked, "Hudson, what's wrong?"

Hudson walked slowly toward her, his eyes glazed over as he grabbed her arm and said in a hoarse voice, "He…he's dead. Terrence is dead."

CHAPTER 16

There was a collective gasp among everyone on the back deck as they all stared at Hudson in shock. Then, when his words finally sunk in, they jumped to their feet and raced up the stairs.

Merrick was still in Terrence's room, his face ashen as he stood over the body. Misty was one of the first to arrive, and when she stepped into the room, she quickly surveyed the scene before her. Terrence was lying face down with a bloody gash on the back of his head. He was facing the bed while his feet pointed toward the door, and Misty noticed a small bloodstain on the corner of his nightstand.

"You're sure he's dead?" she asked Merrick.

Merrick nodded. "Yes," he said softly. "He's stone cold. We both checked his pulse; there is none."

"Oh, good Lord," Evelyn whispered, and Misty turned to find her clutching her husband's arm with one hand over her mouth.

Caleb didn't say a word, nor did Frankie. They both simply stared at the body in cool silence, as Delta pushed her way to the front to get a better look.

"Wow, I didn't know it would happen this soon," Luke breathed, and everyone looked at him questioningly. His eyes wide, he asked, "What? Am I the only one who saw it?"

"Saw what?" Brice asked.

"The black wolf," he said. "I looked out of my window last night, and when the lightning flashed, I saw a black wolf running away from the lodge."

"Wolf or no wolf, it looks like Terrence fell and hit his head on the nightstand," Merrick said in a heavy tone.

"How did he fall?" Misty asked, glancing around the floor. "I don't see anything he could have tripped over."

Merrick crouched on the floor and peered under the bed. "It looks like his flashlight rolled under here," he said, reaching under the bed to grab the light. "Maybe he dropped his flashlight, got disoriented in the dark while trying to find it, and stumbled?"

"He also told us when we went downstairs for the buckets that he felt dizzy from all the smoke," Hudson spoke up. "That could also have caused him to lose his balance."

"Is there ever any clear reason why someone dies after the wolf has been spotted?" Luke asked.

Misty may have thought she saw the wolf, too, but she wasn't buying any of it, especially after hearing someone out in the hallway last night. She decided to hold her peace, though. For now.

"Hudson, let's see if we can drive into town,"

Merrick said, ignoring Luke's question. "I tried calling the sheriff, but I still can't get a call through. I don't know if the roads are blocked or not, but let's at least give it a try."

The two men asked everyone to leave the room, and then they locked the door behind them. The thought of a dead body lying on the other side of that door was unnerving, and everyone looked a bit pale as they quietly headed back downstairs. Misty stopped at her room and nodded at Brice to come inside with her.

"This is crazy, huh?" he asked after she shut the door. "Can you imagine stumbling in the dark and hitting your head like that? As annoying as he seemed to be, I feel bad for him."

"I'm not sure that's what really happened," Misty told him, keeping her voice low.

Brice's eyebrows shot up. "You think someone *killed* him? Misty, that's insane."

"But what about that thump I heard last night?" Misty pressed insistently. "Right after the thump, I heard someone coming out of a room just down the hall from mine…in the direction of Terrence's room! Brice, I think it was the killer. Why else wouldn't they have identified themselves after I called out?"

Brice shook his head and blew out a short, quick breath. "Are you *sure* you heard someone? It was storming and your flashlight went out; maybe it was just thunder you heard."

Planting her hands on her hips, Misty glared at

Brice and said indignantly, "I know what I heard, Brice. If you don't believe me, then fine, but…"

"Okay, okay," Brice interrupted, holding up his hands in surrender. "I believe you. You do realize what you're saying, though, right?"

Misty nodded, sighing. "Yes. This means that someone here at the lodge is a murderer."

Two hours later, Merrick and Hudson returned. The sheriff wasn't with them, and by the looks on their faces when they called everyone into the dining room, their news wasn't good.

"The road is blocked by downed trees and power lines, and a portion of the road looks like it's been washed out," Merrick told everyone, his voice heavy. "We stopped at a neighbor's house along the way, and after a bit, we were finally able to get in contact with the sheriff through their CB radio. He said a tornado came through the area last night and it might be days or even a couple of weeks before the roads are cleared and they can get up here."

"So, what now?" Luke wanted to know. "A dead body can't just lay up there for that long."

"We're running the refrigerators and freezers off of a small generator," Hudson replied. Looking a bit peaked, he swallowed hard and added, "So, we'll have to put…put him in the walk-in cooler until they can get here."

Everyone blinked at his words, and Misty's stomach turned at the thought of a dead body lying in the lodge's cooler. From the look on everyone else's faces, they apparently felt the same way.

"The sheriff told us to keep Terrence's room locked and untouched, so I'd like to ask you all to not enter his room for any reason," Merrick added.

"Why does the sheriff want the room to remain untouched?" Luke asked in a slightly suspicious tone. "Does he think Terrence's death wasn't an accident? Did you tell him about the black wolf?"

"No, to both questions," Merrick replied. "His wanting the room to remain untouched is simply standard procedure."

Everyone went their separate ways then, and while Terrence's body was being moved, Misty and Brice went outside for some fresh air.

"How long do you think we'll be trapped here?" Misty asked as they slowly walked around the property.

Brice shrugged. "Hopefully not that long, but who knows? I'm sure they're going to focus on the main roads in town first before they start on these small mountain roads, so it could definitely be a week or more."

Kicking aside a small branch that was lying in her path, Misty shivered and said, "Let's hope that won't be the case."

"I just hope we'll get some cell service soon," Brice stated with a sigh. "My family is going to wonder what in the world has happened to us."

"They'll be heading up here if they don't hear from us soon," Misty said with a chuckle.

"I wish Luke would quit hammering on about that black wolf," Brice stated in an annoyed tone. "It's silly."

Misty nodded but didn't say anything. She didn't want to admit that she thought she'd seen the wolf as well. Surely, it had just been a figment of her imagination.

Glancing back at the lodge, she chewed on her lip for a moment and said thoughtfully, "I wonder if there's any evidence in Terrence's room that the sheriff might miss."

Glancing over at her, Brice asked, "You mean like fingerprints or something?"

"Not necessarily DNA type of evidence," she replied. "More like something Terrence might have had in his possession that would point to a particular person. Something the police wouldn't notice or think seems suspicious."

"Well, they probably won't be looking for anything like that anyway, since they think it was an accident," Brice pointed out.

Spinning around to face him, Misty grabbed Brice's arm and said, "You've got to help me get into his room."

His eyes flying open wide, Brice shook his head and said, "What? No way! Merrick plainly asked everyone to stay out of his room."

Misty began pulling Brice back in the direction of the lodge, her mind made up. "I know," she stated matter-of-factly, "which is why no one can know what I'm up to. You'll have to be my lookout."

"Nope, nothing doing," Brice said stubbornly, pulling his arm away from her grasp. "Besides, the door will be locked and you're not some professional lock picker…are you?"

Cocking an eyebrow at Brice, Misty replied drolly, "Of course not, but have you seen those old locks? It can't be *that* hard."

Brice rolled his eyes. "I'm still not helping you."

Pursing her lips in annoyance, Misty shrugged and said, "Fine. I'll do it myself."

CHAPTER 17

Brice finally caved, and after Misty was certain that everyone was downstairs in the dining room eating lunch, she grabbed a bobby pin and headed to Terrence's room.

"If you hear me start to whistle, you'd better get out of there," Brice told her from his lookout point near the stairs.

Nodding, Misty slipped her hands into the work gloves she'd found in Brice's truck and began working on the lock. It took a whole of twenty seconds for the lock to pop open, and with a satisfied smile, Misty turned the knob and slid inside.

She stood still for a moment, her eyes taking in the bloodstain on the rug and the mussed-up bed. Apparently, Terrence had already been in bed and got up to…what? Use the bathroom? Or had he heard something and gone to investigate? The clothes he'd been wearing the day before were draped across a chair, and Misty spotted a toiletry bag sitting on the bathroom counter.

Reminding herself to hurry, Misty headed for the suitcase first. It seemed that Terrence hadn't done much unpacking; his clothes were folded in a neat pile and his shoes were stacked to one side. Her eyes fell upon a manila envelope tucked into the inside zip pocket, and she carefully pulled it out.

The contents of the envelope immediately piqued her interest. Inside was a newspaper article about Jackson Dagon's death, along with a handful of photographs. Misty flipped through the photos, which appeared to have been taken on the camping trip the six friends took together after graduation. Wanting to have time to study over everything later, Misty withdrew Brice's cell phone from her pocket and began snapping pictures, since her own phone was dead.

She'd just taken the last picture when she suddenly heard the sound of a whistled tune echoing down the hall. Her heart catching, she quickly put everything back in its place and closed the suitcase. The whistling grew louder, and Misty knew she needed to get out of the room as quickly as possible.

Tucking Brice's phone back into her pocket, Misty opened the door and peered out into the hallway. She could hear footsteps coming up the staircase, and Brice was waving frantically at her from his bedroom door. Nodding at him, Misty quickly locked Terrence's door and slipped down the back stairs, hoping Delta wouldn't be in the hallway just outside of the kitchen and ask what she was doing.

The small hallway was empty, and Misty slipped quietly past the kitchen and out into the main room. It seemed that everyone was still in the dining room eating, and making certain to act nonchalant, Misty walked through the lodge and back up the main staircase.

"I thought we were goners for sure," Brice told her a moment later when she entered his room.

"Well, thankfully we weren't caught, so it's all good," she told him with a satisfied smile. Pulling his phone from her pocket, she waved it in the air and said, "I just may have gotten that evidence I was hoping for."

His eyebrows shooting upward, Brice asked, "Really? What did you find?"

They both settled on the sofa while Misty unlocked the phone and retrieved the photos she'd taken.

"I'm not sure yet, but don't you find it odd that Terrence had all this stuff in his suitcase?" she asked, showing the pictures to Brice.

"Maybe he just wanted to reminisce?"

Cocking an eyebrow, Misty asked drolly, "About the night their best friend died?"

"You do have a point," Brice replied as he looked over Misty's shoulder at the pictures.

There were about fifteen photos, all taken on the camping trip. Some were of the whole group, one was of Frankie and Evelyn about to jump into the lake, and a few were of just the guys. When Misty came to one photograph in particular, she stopped, her head tilting to the side as she studied it.

"What's wrong?" Brice asked.

Misty shook her head. "I'm not entirely sure,"

she muttered. "Does that expression look like a jealous one to you?"

Brice leaned forward to take a closer look. "Yes, it does," he agreed. "In most of the pictures, everyone is happy and smiling, but not this one. I'd say by the clenched jaw and scowl, there was definitely some jealousy there."

Swiping to the next picture, Misty realized she'd reached the last one, which was the article written about Jackson's death. Her eyes skimmed over the words as she read softly under her breath, and she stopped when she reached a certain quote.

"Listen to this," she told Brice as she read aloud. "When the sheriff questioned the others, Frankie, Hudson, and Merrick said they didn't hear Jackson leave the camp. Evelyn said she thought she heard something, but went back to sleep, and Terrence said he was positive he heard the sound of two people arguing. When the police asked who it was and what they were saying, Terrence simply said he didn't know."

"Didn't you say Terrence seemed to be harassing Evelyn?" Brice asked. When Misty nodded, he continued, "I'm thinking he knew more than he let on to the sheriff all those years ago and came back to blackmail someone. What I can't figure, though, is why he waited this long."

Misty thought about it for a moment and said, "It could be he needs money since he's going through a divorce. Maybe his ex-wife is trying to take more than he was willing to give."

"I think you've hit on it, Miss Raven," Brice said. "Now, how do we prove it?"

"By being nosy," Misty stated. "Are you willing to help, Watson?"

With a twinkle in his eyes, Brice saluted and said, "Take the lead, Sherlock."

CHAPTER 18

Tori

When Tuesday morning arrived, Tori and her family went down to the police station to see Dylan.

"I don't have any updates on the case," he said as soon as he saw them.

"We're not here about my case," Tori told him. "We're here because we're worried about Brice and Misty. They were supposed to come home yesterday but never showed, and we can't reach them on their cellphones."

"We heard that the storms were really bad in the Dahlonega area, and we're very concerned," Amy added, her forehead wrinkled with worry.

"Is there any way you can get in contact with the sheriff up there and see if he's heard anything?" Neil wanted to know.

Dylan nodded. "Give me a few minutes and I'll see what I can do."

They all waited in the front lobby, their stomachs clenched with worry. Pops got up and paced around the room, his hands stuffed into the pockets of his pants, and Neil's leg jiggled up and down incessantly.

"They said they had bad reception up on the mountain," Tori told them for at least the third time that morning. "Maybe the storm knocked out what little they had."

"But why not come home?" Pops asked. "Unless there was an accident or…"

"Maybe the roads are blocked and they can't get out yet," Neil interrupted him.

"I hope that's all it is," Amy said softly.

Since Brice's dad died and his mom moved away, he'd become more like a brother to Tori and a son to her parents than a cousin and nephew. They all loved him dearly, and even though they hadn't known Misty but for a few short months, she'd become a part of their family. The possibility of something bad happening to either…or both…of them was something Tori wouldn't even let herself think about.

Dylan poked his head into the lobby and waved at the four of them to come back into his office. They all jumped to their feet and hurried after him, and once seated in the chairs across from his desk, they waited nervously to hear what he had to say.

"I finally got in contact with the sheriff in Dahlonega, and he said the storm left downed trees and power lines all over that area," he told them. There was something in the tone of his voice and the way he kept looking away that set alarm bells off in Tori's mind. "He said he's actually spoken with the owners of the lodge, and although they are currently trapped on the mountain, everyone is alright. Except…except for one guest."

Everyone leaned toward him, their hands clutching the arms on the chairs as they waited for him to continue. Tori swallowed past the lump in her throat as she fought against the hot tears that threatened to choke her.

"Who…who is the one guest?" she asked in a hoarse tone.

Dylan shook his head and sighed. "I don't know. The sheriff didn't get his name."

"*His* name?" Pops rasped. "What happened?"

Meeting their gazes head-on, Dylan said, "He's dead."

The Barlows stared at Dylan in stunned silence. After a moment, Amy burst into tears as Pops stood and began pacing again. Tori simply sat there with wide eyes.

"What happened to him?" Neil finally asked, his voice tight.

"I don't know all the details; the sheriff doesn't either until he can get some men up there, but I believe it was an accidental death," Dylan replied. Looking around at everyone, he added, "We don't know that it's Brice. I'm sure there were several guests staying at the lodge, so it could have been anyone."

They all nodded, each hoping that he was right. Tori couldn't imagine anything happening to

Brice. Life just wouldn't be the same without him.

"You'll let us know the moment you hear anything?" Pops asked.

Dylan nodded. "Yes, sir. I promise."

The Barlows thanked him and left, their silence heavy as they walked outside. Not wanting to go home just yet, Tori said, "I'm going to the shop for a little while."

When everyone looked at her in surprise, she added, "I can't let Julian Cooper rule my life. I've got to go back to work sometime, and it might as well be now. Besides, I think a distraction will be good for me right now."

"Call us if you need anything, honey," her mom said, reaching out to touch her arm.

Squeezing her hand, Tori promised she would. After giving Pops a kiss on the cheek, she told everyone goodbye and drove down the street to her shop. She left the closed sign out while she did a bit of baking, and as she worked, all she could think about was Brice. How long would they have to wait before they would know anything? It was killing her not knowing.

With everything that had happened the last few days, Tori felt as if the weight of the world was on her shoulders. After she finished with the baking, she quickly cleaned the tables out front and opened the shop to begin serving her customers.

"Tori, I'm surprised to see you back at work so soon," Patrick Donovan said as soon as he stepped inside. "Are you sure you're up to it?"

Taking a deep breath, Tori opened her mouth to say yes but instead ended up spilling everything about Brice and Misty. By the time she'd finished, she was crying all over again. So much for getting her mind off things.

His face filled with concern, Mr. Donovan reached out to pat her hand. "Tori, I am so sorry," he said. "Please let me know the instant y'all hear anything."

With a sniff, Tori nodded and said, "I will." Clearing her throat, she forced a smile and changed the subject before she was in a complete puddle of tears. "I made those chocolate chip cappuccino muffins you like so much," she told him. "Would you like one?"

His eyes brightening, Mr. Donovan said, "I would love one! Actually, make it two."

Not long after Mr. Donovan left, Dylan Mitchell walked in, and Tori felt her breath catch in her chest. Did he have news of Brice?

"I haven't heard anything yet," he immediately told her, and she deflated like a balloon. "I just came by to check on you. There's been no sign of Cooper, has there?"

"I haven't really been paying much attention," she told him as she placed a dozen freshly baked cookies inside the display cabinet. "I've been too distracted by the shop and worrying about Brice and Misty. I haven't noticed anything strange, though."

Tapping his fingers on the counter for a moment,

Dylan finally asked, "Do you know any self-defense moves?"

Tori looked at him in surprise. "No." She shook her head. "Unless running counts?"

Dylan's lips twitched, and Tori realized that was the closest she'd ever seen him smile.

"No, that does not count," he replied. "Why don't you come by the station when you get off work? We have a training room there, and I'd feel a lot better if I knew you might be able to defend yourself if Cooper confronts you again."

Tori was a bit caught off guard by the thoughtful and generous offer, and she stumbled around for a moment before finally agreeing to meet him later. "Thank you, Officer Mitchell. I really appreciate this."

"Think nothing of it," he replied. "And call me Dylan. See you later?"

Tori nodded and waved goodbye as he walked out the door. Her cell phone chimed just then, and she snatched it up, hoping it was from Brice or Misty. When she saw it was from Chris, she felt surprised yet again. He hadn't texted her at all yesterday, and she assumed she'd heard the last from him again. Apparently, she was wrong.

CHAPTER 19

Misty

Tuesday morning, Misty went downstairs and was surprised to find that Brice hadn't come down yet. She considered going back up to knock on his door but was distracted when Luke stepped up beside her and poked her with his elbow.

"I hope we won't find any more dead bodies this morning," he quipped.

"I hope not," Misty said. Glancing over at Luke, she casually asked, "Did you know Terrence?"

Luke shook his head. "No, I didn't. He left town right before I was born."

Misty found it a little strange that he knew the exact date Terrence left town, but simply summed it up to the whole ordeal surrounding Jackson's death most likely being a big deal in the town. Dahlonega wasn't a large place, and it would have been even smaller almost thirty years ago. She imagined people still talked about the young man who fell to his death on Devil's Cliff.

"Really?" Misty asked as she followed Luke out to the back deck. "I thought I saw the two of you talking at the bonfire."

Luke blinked in surprise. "Oh, uh, yes, we were discussing work," he stammered. "He'd heard about my computer business and was asking about it. I hadn't met him, though, before then."

"I see," Misty replied.

Greeting Delta, who was back at her station beside the grill, Misty filled a bowl with oatmeal and headed toward a table. Brice stepped outside then, and as Luke went over to speak to him, Misty sat down by herself while the two men fixed their plates. Hudson was sitting at the table next to hers, and he pleasantly wished her a good morning.

"Is Frankie not joining you this morning?" Misty asked him.

Hudson shook his head. "No, I'm afraid she has a headache. Terrence's death has just upset her terribly, so I told her to stay in bed today and rest."

Frankie, upset about Terrence's death? Misty was surprised to hear that. She was also shocked to know that anything could bother Frankie's nerves, as the woman seemed to be as hard as nails. Perhaps Misty had been wrong about her.

"I was told y'all hadn't seen him since he left after Jackson Dagon's death several years ago?" Misty asked nonchalantly.

Hudson was pouring cream into his coffee, and Misty noticed he spilled a bit as soon as she mentioned Jackson's name.

"Uh, yes, that's right," he replied, shifting slightly in his seat. "He got a job offer that summer, one that he just couldn't refuse."

"It's a little strange that he never came back to visit, though, don't you think?"

Hudson hesitated, glancing at Misty with a look in his eyes that she couldn't quite decipher. "That's just Terrence for you," he finally replied with a small, forced laugh. "He never really cared for anyone but himself."

"And yet you all were pretty close before he left?" Misty pressed.

"He liked to think we were," Hudson stated with a tight smile. Clearing his throat, he quickly added, "I'm not trying to talk bad about the deceased, and I feel terrible that this has happened to Terrence. I hope you understand that."

Misty nodded. "Of course."

Brice and Luke joined her then, and Hudson left pretty soon afterward.

"I'll be at the front desk if anyone needs me," he told them all before hurrying away.

"What's wrong with him?" Brice asked, watching as he walked away. "He acts nervous or upset about something."

Misty shrugged innocently. "Who knows?"

Brice was right, though; Hudson *had* acted a little on edge after their conversation. Had Misty somehow struck a nerve with him?

After breakfast, Merrick and Hudson announced they were going out to start clearing the trails behind the lodge. As everyone was bored and had nothing else to do, they all asked if they could help.

"How kind," Merrick stated with a broad smile. "With all the extra hands, maybe it won't take as long to get them cleared."

After changing into something more fitting for what Misty referred to as "yard work", she and Brice joined the others out on the trails. Merrick was right; the trails were a mess. Tree limbs were strewn everywhere, with piles of leaves and debris scattered all along the path. Everyone eventually branched out and went their separate ways, each taking a section of the many different trails. Misty and Brice ended up by themselves, far away from the others, and Misty enjoyed the ease between them as they worked. It was nice to get away from everyone else for a while and just breathe.

"You're a hard worker, Miss Raven," Brice told her as he gritted his teeth and shoved a large branch out of the path.

Misty was pushing leaves and pine straw into a paper bag that was nearly as tall as she was, and she jokingly tossed a pine cone at Brice. "Thanks," she replied with a smile. "You're not too bad yourself."

Catching the pine cone in his gloved hand, Brice raised his eyebrows and said, "Oh, you don't want to have a pine cone fight with me. I'm the king of pine cone fights."

"Is a pine cone fight in the south the equivalent of a snowball fight up north?" she asked, laughing as she threw a handful of leaves into his face.

Taking off his gloves, Brice grabbed her around the waist and began tickling her mercilessly. With a screech, Misty began twisting and squirming like a wildcat, trying unsuccessfully to get away from the torture, but she was soon laughing too hard to make much progress. Clutching Brice's hands, Misty begged him to stop.

"I surrender!" She gasped, still laughing. "No more pine cone fights, I promise."

Brice stopped, a grin on his handsome face as he looked down at her. Both of their chests were heaving from their little wrestling match, and when Brice slowly wound his fingers around hers, Misty suddenly realized how close they were standing. He released one of her hands to pull a piece of pine straw from her hair, his eyes warm as he gently touched her on the cheek. Feeling dizzy, Misty simply stared up at him, her whole body warm all over as Brice slowly began to lean toward her.

Just then, an odd rumble sounded from within the trees, and the spell between them was broken. Misty and Brice spun around, their eyes searching the thick woods that surrounded them on either side. Straight ahead and to their left, the bushes began to sway and tremble, and the snapping of twigs and branches could be heard amongst the thick brush.

"Brice, what is it?" Misty whispered, clutching his arm.

Brice took her hand and began to back away slowly. "I don't know," he replied, "but I think we'd better get out of here."

The tone in his voice sent chills down Misty's spine, and she clenched his fingers tightly within hers. They began hurrying back down the trail the way they'd come, but when they reached a fork, they suddenly realized they didn't know which way to turn. The storm had blown down all the signs, and both of them were so engrossed in their work that neither could remember if they'd turned left or right. Both trails had been cleared, that much was obvious, but which would lead to where the others were working?

"Which way?" she asked, her breath catching when another rumble sounded once again from the trees, much closer this time. "Maybe either trail will lead us to *someone.* If the others are even still working; it's gotten later than I realized."

"Let's try this one," Brice said, and they took off down the right-hand fork.

The trail was rough and uneven, and Misty could hear her heart pounding in her ears as they ran. She kept looking back over her shoulder, waiting to see if whatever it was would leap from the bushes and attack. Was it the black wolf? Did such a creature even exist here in these mountains? She was quite sure that wolves, or at least coyotes, lived in this area; the howls she'd heard in the night were proof of that. But would a lone wolf or coyote make such deep, guttural sounds? Suddenly, she recalled what Brice said about Luke's grandfather tracking the bear over the mountain, and her breath caught. Could a bear be after them?

Misty's legs were beginning to grow weak, and she could feel Brice's palm sweating against her own. The trail seemed to be never-ending when suddenly, just up ahead, a bend appeared. What if no one was on the other side of that bend? What if they had to turn around and go back to face whatever awaited them in the woods?

A growl suddenly sounded in the trees right next to Misty, and her foot caught on a protruding root. With a loud scream, she was sent spiraling forward, her hands reaching out to grasp at Brice for help. He caught her and snatched her to the other side of the trail, where they both stopped and faced the trees, their chests heaving from the exertion. Brice pushed Misty behind him and grabbed a big stick, his shoulders rigged and his stance ready to face anything.

The sound of retreating footsteps as they crashed through the forest met their ears, and Misty leaned against Brice for a moment, trying to calm the racing of her heart.

"I guess it's gone?" she asked hopefully.

"I think your scream must have scared it away," Brice said. Looking down at her, he gently pushed her hair back from her face and asked, "Are you okay?"

Misty nodded. "Yes, I'm okay. Let's just please find the others."

It seemed that everyone had returned to the lodge for lunch, and just as they'd hoped, the lodge could be seen up ahead once they rounded the bend in the trail.

"There you two are," Hudson greeted them as soon as they stepped inside. "We were just about to come looking for you. Delta has sandwiches in the dining room."

"Hudson, are there any dangerous, wild animals around here?" Brice asked him, quickly explaining what had happened.

"Oh, it was probably just a young bear who was curious about the two of you," he told them, waving a hand in the air. "Or maybe an animal was injured during the storm. We never have wild animal attacks around here, though, so I doubt you were in any real danger."

Rubbing her arms, Misty shrugged and said, "Maybe so. I guess us city slickers were just a little jumpy out there in the woods."

Cocking an eyebrow, Brice stated drolly, "I'm not exactly a city slicker, thank you."

Misty laughed. "You co-own a hardware store, Brice," she said jokingly. "You're not exactly Daniel Boone either."

As they headed for the dining room, Misty spotted Frankie coming in through the front door with Luke. Both of their clothes were dirty, and a leaf was protruding from Frankie's hair. They stood in a corner in deep conversation, and Misty stared at them for a moment, her brow wrinkling slightly.

"What's wrong?" Brice asked.

"Hudson said Frankie had a headache and was planning to stay in bed all day," Misty replied. "I guess she must be feeling better now."

CHAPTER 20

Tori

After a long day at the shop, Tori was even more exhausted than before. She was thankful, though, to have the distraction. The less she thought about Julian Cooper and Brice and Misty, the less tense and stressed she felt. It was always at the back of her mind, though, and every time the bell above the door rang, she jumped a little.

When Penny's boyfriend, Theo, walked into the shop, Tori was surprised. She normally only saw him at church with Penny; he'd never come into the shop before.

"Hi, Theo," she greeted him as she wiped off the tables. "Is Penny with you?"

"No," he replied. He went to the display case and bent over to look at the selection inside. "I'm going to pick her up later for dinner. It's her birthday, you know."

Tori tucked the hand towel into her apron and walked to stand behind the counter. "No, I didn't know that," she said. "If you'd like to get a cookie or something, I can decorate it for you."

"I think I'll just take a few of those cake pops,"

he said, pointing to the chocolate-coated dessert. While Tori grabbed a box, he looked around the shop. "Nice place you have here," he added.

"Thanks," Tori replied. Attempting to make polite conversation while she packaged the cake pops, she asked, "So, you're from Savannah?"

Theo's gaze quickly swung in her direction, his eyes narrowing slightly. "Who told you that?" He wanted to know. "Penny?"

Tori blinked at the sharpness in his tone. "No, I heard it around town," she replied, adding with a sheepish shrug, "Small town, you know? News gets around."

Theo stared at her for a moment, his expression tight. Finally, he cracked a small smile and said, "I know what you mean. Yes, I live in Savannah."

As Theo paid for the cake pops, Tori said, "I hope you and Penny enjoy those. Tell her I said happy birthday?"

When Theo handed Tori the money, his fingers brushed against hers, and she glanced up at him, feeling a little startled. He was staring at her, his black eyes piercing and unsettling. Tori quickly pulled the money from his fingers and gathered his change, uncertain of what it was about him that made her feel so uncomfortable.

As Tori handed him his change, Theo finally answered her question. "Yes, I'll tell her you said happy birthday," he stated, and with that, he left the shop.

Tori sighed as she watched him leave, feeling

tired and on edge. It was starting to get late, so she decided to close the shop early and head to the police station to meet Dylan. Once she locked the front door, put out the "closed" sign, and turned off all the lights, the silence of the shop seemed to ring in her ears. She walked through the front room into the kitchen and untied her apron, glancing at her reflection in one of the hanging pots.

"Oh, dear," she muttered when she saw her mussed hair and the flour smeared on her cheek.

Hurrying into the bathroom, she quickly washed her face and touched up her hair. She was so preoccupied that she almost didn't hear the creak that came from the front room. With a can of hairspray clutched in her hand, she froze, listening intently. Was the creak simply caused by the old building as it settled, or was someone out there?

You locked the front door, she told herself. *Plus, it's still light outside. No one is going to break into your shop in broad daylight.*

Still, she couldn't get the niggling prick of fear in her mind to subside, and she turned off the bathroom light and waited. There it was again; another creak. Grasping the hairspray in her hand to use as a weapon, Tori slid behind the bathroom door and peered out through the crack. If the kitchen door opened, should she scream? Run at the intruder with the hairspray?

No, she thought. *Just stay where you are. Maybe he won't see you.*

She waited for what seemed like an interminable

amount of time, but nothing happened. Had she imagined the creak? Maybe she was losing it. She'd just stepped from behind the bathroom door when another creak met her ears. Her eyes flew to her purse, which rested several feet away on the kitchen counter, and she lunged forward, hoping to get to her phone and call for help.

With her heart in her throat, Tori raced across the kitchen. The space that separated her from the counter stretched out like an ocean or a vast desert, and as slow as her trembling legs were moving, it might as well have been a million miles instead of just a few mere feet. There was suddenly another creak; she heard it as loudly as if it had been put over a loudspeaker, and her breath caught.

In a matter of seconds, Tori reached her purse and snatched it up, quickly pushing her hand inside as she searched frantically for the phone. When her fingers finally found it, she pulled it out and froze. Who should she call? The police? Her parents? What would she tell them? That someone was in the shop?

With shaking fingers, Tori unlocked the phone and was about to call Dylan when she suddenly realized the intruder had yet to show himself. Was she overreacting? Surely if someone was out there, he'd have already made himself known. What if she called Dylan for no reason? Turning slowly to look at the kitchen door, she gathered her courage and swallowed past the lump in her throat as she took a tentative step forward.

One step, then two. Her heart was pounding so fiercely she felt as if she couldn't breathe. What would she do if Julian Cooper was in the other room, waiting for her? Holding the can of hairspray out in front of herself, she threw open the kitchen door and peered out into the main room.

All was still and quiet, just as she'd left it. She quickly flipped on the lights and looked around, seeing no one. The front door was still shut tightly, and through the windows, Tori could see cars and people passing by, one of which was Noah Welch. He glanced into the shop and waved when he saw her, and she forced a smile and waved back.

With a sigh, Tori lowered the can and slumped back against the wall, feeling very silly for allowing her emotions to get the better of her. In the few hours she'd known him, Julian Cooper had turned her into a trembling, frightened woman who jumped at every little sound, and she didn't like it. Not one bit.

Squaring her shoulders, Tori spun on her heel and returned to the kitchen, where she snatched up her purse and headed out the back door. She was going to learn those self-defense moves and would hopefully start feeling comfortable in her own skin again.

When Tori arrived at the police station, her resolve had already begun to weaken. Could a few little moves really protect her during a life and death situation? She wasn't sure but was still determined to give it a try. After all, what could it hurt?

Feeling a bit awkward, Tori peered into Dylan's office and waved at him. "Is now not a good time?" she asked when she saw the large stack of papers in front of him.

"Now is actually the perfect time," he replied, blowing out a sigh as he tossed his pen onto the desk. "I need a break."

Tori followed Dylan down a very long hallway, nodding and smiling at the other officers as they passed. They finally reached a metal door, which Dylan held open for Tori, and she saw that it was a large conference room the men had apparently turned into a gym of sorts. There was a large mat in the center, a couple of benches with various-sized weights beside them, a rowing machine, and several other machines Tori didn't recognize.

"It doesn't look like it now, but we use this room quite often," Dylan stated as he closed the door behind them. "It's a good way to blow off some steam. Plus, when things are slow, we can come work out for a bit." Glancing at Tori's dress, Dylan cleared his throat and asked, "Do you have anything you can change into? I don't think a dress will be…well…I don't think it will work for the moves I'd like to show you."

Her cheeks flushing, Tori stammered, "I, uh, didn't bring anything else. I can just come back tomorrow…"

Holding up his hand, Dylan shook his head and said, "Give me a minute. I'll be right back."

Seconds later, he returned carrying a gym bag. "I know they'll be big on you, but you can tie the string at the waist," he said, pulling out a t-shirt and pair of sweatpants. When Tori just stared at them in silence, he quickly added, "They're clean. I promise."

Feeling even more awkward, Tori silently took the clothes and went into the bathroom to change. After tying the pants as tightly as possible, she slid into the t-shirt and emerged from the bathroom. She noticed Dylan had taken his uniform shirt off and was now wearing his white undershirt, revealing a set of very broad shoulders.

"I'm ready," she told him.

Nodding, Dylan instructed her to follow him to the center of the mat and lie down on her back. Tori did as he asked without question, but when he squatted down and straddled her, she blinked in surprise.

"When a man attacks a woman, this is something he'll do quite often," he told her. Taking her wrists, he gently pinned them above her head. "If this ever happens, the first thing I want you to do is to make sure his face is directly above yours; scoot your body forward or backward if you have to. Once you're in position, plant your feet on the ground and shove your pelvis upward. Give it a try."

Nodding, Tori did as he asked, not expecting her

move to send him spiraling forward. He released her wrists to catch himself, and then said, "What you do now is very important. I want you to slide your arms quickly down to your side and wrap them around my waist, keeping the side of your face flush against my chest."

Concentrating on what he'd just said, Tori slid her arms down from above her head, wrapped them around his torso, and pressed her face against his body.

Wow, he smells good, she thought, and then immediately scolded herself for getting distracted.

"Now, shimmy yourself up, wrap one arm around mine, and pull my arm inward, knocking me off balance. After you do that, you'll use your opposite leg and arm to flip us both over."

Tori had to try the last few moves several times before she could pull it off, but once she did, she was suddenly lying on top of Dylan and staring directly into his face.

"I did it!" She cried with excitement.

"Good job," he congratulated her. "Let's do it a few more times, and each time, try to move a little faster."

Tori grew faster and faster with each try, and by the time Dylan gave her a high-five and said that was enough for one night, she was exhausted.

"Come back tomorrow and I'll show you the next one," he told her.

Out of breath but otherwise feeling great, Tori nodded and said, "Sounds good. Thanks for doing this, Dylan."

Smiling, Dylan said, "You're very welcome. I've got to make sure the owner of my favorite bakery stays in business."

Tori laughed. "I've never asked before, but what do you do with all the treats you buy from me?"

"I take them to various places," he replied. "Sometimes I'll drop them off at the fire station or give them to the staff at the medical clinic, and other times I'll hand them out to the men here at the station. Everyone raves about how delicious everything is."

Tori blinked, her heart warming at his kindness. "What a thoughtful gesture," she said. "You truly are a servant of the public, aren't you, Officer Mitchell?"

Looking a little embarrassed, Dylan shrugged and said, "Oh, it's nothing. I enjoy doing it."

After she'd changed her clothes, Dylan walked Tori to her car and they said their goodbyes. As she drove away, Tori wondered how she'd known him all these months but hadn't realized what a kind heart rested beneath Officer Mitchell's badge. Sometimes, people surprise you.

As Tori headed toward her parents' home, she failed to notice the car that turned out of the police station and slowly drove behind her.

CHAPTER 21

Misty

With all the wood from the fallen limbs and branches they'd chopped and gathered from the trails, Merrick and Hudson decided to do another bonfire Tuesday night for them all. Delta once again brought out the s'mores and hot chocolate, and even though Terrence's death still lingered in the back of everyone's mind, it was nice to have something fun to do.

The evening was cool, and the stars were brighter than Misty had ever seen. It was so calm and peaceful that it was hard to imagine such a terrible storm had just passed through. It was also hard to believe a dead body was lying inside the lodge's cooler

"Having a nice time?"

Misty turned to find Merrick taking a seat on the bale of pine straw beside hers. Brice and Luke were playing a game of Cornhole right next to the fire's light, while everyone watched and cheered them on.

Nodding her head in response to Merrick's question, Misty said, "Yes, I am. Now that the storm is gone, this is perfect weather to enjoy the outdoors.”

Taking a sip of his hot chocolate, Merrick readily agreed. After a moment of comfortable silence, he glanced over at her and asked, “Have you been able to gather any information on your mother?”

Misty sighed and looked down at her hands. “A bit, but not nearly what I was hoping for.” Her eyes brightening, she looked up and added, “But Luke said his mother and Elena were good friends, and he has some old photos and letters they wrote to each other. Once we get back down the mountain, he’s going to give them to me.”

“That’s wonderful news! I completely forgot about how close the two of them were,” Merrick replied. Glancing down at his now empty mug, he added, “Frankie told me you’re trying to find out who your father is.”

“I am, but it’s starting to seem rather hopeless,” Misty told him. “But maybe I’ll find something in those old pictures and letters that Luke has.”

His eyes blinking thoughtfully, Merrick tilted his head to the side and said, “You know, I’m pretty sure I’ve got some old pictures on the top shelf of my closet that may include Elena. Give me a minute; I’ll be right back.”

Misty waited with nervous anticipation for Merrick to return. When he did, he was carrying an old shoebox full of photographs.

“I don’t know why I didn’t think of this before,” he said as he sat back down and placed the shoebox on his knee. He dug through the photos for a moment, a look of nostalgia softening his features as he paused and studied a few of them. Holding one up to the light, he said, "I remember this night like it was only last week. Our group of friends went out for pizza one weekend about two or three months before graduation, and I remember I ate an entire large pie myself on a dare. I was so sick that I couldn't eat for two whole days after that."

Laughing, Misty took the offered photo and studied it closely. "My goodness, Mr. Merrick, you were even more handsome then than you are now," she told him.

Merrick blushed and shook his head. "I think this dim lighting has your eyesight a bit blurry," he said.

Misty pointed to the man on Merrick's left and asked, "Is that Jackson Dagon?"

Leaning closer to get a better look, Merrick nodded. "Yes, that's him. He was something else. That's Frankie next to him."

"Did the two of them date?" Misty asked, curiously.

Merrick glanced across the fire at Frankie, as if to make certain she wasn't listening. "No," he replied, his voice lower than it had been before. "I always thought she had a crush on him, but she'd never admit it. If Jackson would have ever asked her out, though, I think she would have jumped at the chance to date him."

As she continued to study the picture, Misty's

eyebrows raised slightly. Jackson may have never actually asked Frankie out, but the flirtatious gleam in his eye and the way his arm was draped around Frankie's shoulders for the picture made Misty think he might have led her on.

"Where is Evelyn in this picture?" Misty wanted to know, also making certain to keep her voice low. She didn't want to involve the others just now.

Shrugging, Merrick shuffled through some of the other pictures until he found one with Evelyn. "There she is," he stated, showing Misty. "This looks like the same night, so she must have been in the restroom or something."

Looking at the newest photo, Misty immediately noticed how close Evelyn stood to Terrence, and she suddenly realized that Terrence hadn't been in the first picture either. Had the two ridden together? Or perhaps they'd snuck off in the middle of the pizza party to have a few moments alone.

"I heard that both Terrence and Jackson were interested in Evelyn," Misty stated.

Merrick snickered slightly. "Yeah, they were always in competition with each other. Terrence actually broke up with Alice when he found out Jackson was after Evelyn."

"Alice…was that Delta's sister?"

"Yes, that's right," Merrick replied, nodding. "She would hang out with us sometimes when she was dating Terrence; such a nice girl. After their father died, she just…couldn't handle living any longer. I always felt so terrible about it. If I'd realized how badly she was struggling, I might have been able to help her somehow."

Merrick's eyes were so full of sadness as he spoke that Misty wondered why he **hadn't** reached out to Alice. It was obvious he'd thought a great deal of her; enough so that he'd even hired her sister to work at the lodge.

After a moment, Merrick shook himself and continued going through the photographs. He had a few from the infamous camping trip, and when Misty spotted Hudson standing next to Frankie, she asked Merrick how long they'd been dating.

"Oh, not long," Merrick replied. "He was always such a sucker for Frankie. I was rather surprised when she finally gave in and agreed to date him."

"Why weren't **you** dating anyone?" she asked jokingly.

Merrick looked at her and smiled. "I wanted to be," he said, "but she just wouldn't…"

Before he could finish, a sharp tone spoke out, "Why on earth are you going through those old pictures?"

Glancing up, Misty saw Frankie glaring at her brother as she walked toward him.

Merrick stared back at her for a moment, the look on his face speaking volumes. Apparently, he didn't appreciate the interruption, or the scolding tone in his sister's voice.

"I was looking to see if I could find any of

Elena," he stated coolly. "Do you mind?"

Brice and Luke stopped playing their game, and Misty realized everyone was staring at the twins. Much to her surprise, Frankie backed down and didn't say another word; she simply stomped inside the lodge and slammed the door behind her. Clearing his throat, Hudson stood and hurried after her.

"I'm sorry about that," Merrick said to Misty as everyone slowly began getting back to what they were doing. "She hates revisiting the past."

"Why is that?" Misty wanted to know.

"Jackson's death was hard on her," he replied. "It was hard on all of us. He was a very good friend."

Misty didn't say anything else about it or ask any more questions. A moment later, Merrick's eyes brightened, and he quickly pulled a picture from the stack.

"Here you go," he said proudly, handing her the photograph. "I thought I had one of her."

Taking the picture, Misty held it carefully in both hands like a precious jewel as she tilted it toward the light. The photo was taken in almost the exact spot that Misty and the rest of the group were now occupying. Elena and Merrick were seated on a quilt that had been spread out on the grass. There were books and papers scattered all around, and Elena was smiling happily up at the camera. She was breathtakingly beautiful; even more so than in the photo Mrs. Sanchez had given her. She looked carefree and relaxed as the mountain breeze blew her hair over her shoulders, and Misty spotted *Jane Eyre* resting beside her.

"Were y'all studying, or pleasure reading?" she asked, discreetly wiping her eyes.

Merrick laughed. "Oh, we were studying, but I had forgotten how much she loved that book," he replied, a warm smile on his face. "She constantly talked about it and how she could relate to Jane Eyre."

Misty glanced at him curiously. "How so?"

Shrugging, Merrick replied, "I don't know for sure, but I remember she said once that she knew how it felt to have a troubled childhood and that she understood Jane's reluctance to get close to people. When I tried to ask her about it, she changed the subject. She was very private about her past."

"There are so many things I wish I could ask her," Misty said with a forlorn sigh.

With a sympathetic pat on her shoulder, Merrick said, "I know. I'm sorry I can't help you more."

Pressing the picture to her chest, Misty said, "You have helped tremendously, Mr. Merrick. Thank you. Would you mind if I had a copy made of this picture?"

"Oh, just keep it," he said with a small wave of his hand. "It belongs to you."

Thanking him again, Misty was about to take the picture inside and put it somewhere safe when Evelyn announced she wanted to play Cornhole and stood up. Her jewelry caught the reflection of the fire's light, and Misty wondered once again what Caleb did for a living. Turning back to Merrick, Misty asked him about it.

"He's an accountant," Merrick replied. "I hope the company he works for will understand about his absence."

Her brow wrinkling, Misty asked, "Does Evelyn work?" When Merrick shook his head, Misty muttered, "That's surprising."

"I assume you're referring to her expensive taste in clothes and jewelry?"

"Yes, I thought maybe they were both doctors or lawyers or something," she replied with a sheepish shrug.

"I've always wondered how Caleb could afford to buy all of that for her," Merrick said. "Plus, they have a daughter they're putting through college."

"Maybe they won the lottery and didn't tell anyone," Misty joked.

After losing the game to Luke and relinquishing his place to Evelyn, Brice reclaimed his seat on Misty's other side. Nodding to them both, Merrick stood and went back inside, carrying the shoebox of pictures with him.

"What was that all about?" Brice asked, nodding toward Merrick's retreating figure. "His sister didn't seem too happy with him."

Handing Brice the picture of her mother, Misty explained about Merrick's shoebox full of memories.

"Wow, what a beauty," he breathed as he looked at the picture. "No wonder Hudson said all the men wanted to date her."

Looking over his shoulder at the photo, Misty smiled and said, "She really was beautiful, wasn't she? I wish I could have known her."

Brice handed the picture back to Misty, his eyes warm as he said, "At least you know more now than you did a year ago. I'm proud of you, Misty, for not giving up. She would be proud of you, too."

Suddenly feeling an overwhelming amount of emotions flooding over her, Misty stayed silent for a moment, her throat too tight to speak. Finally, she gave Brice a wobbly smile and whispered, "Thank you. That means so much." Clearing her throat, she stood up and said, "Well, I think I'm going to take a shower and go to bed. Aren't we all glad the lodge has a gas water heater so we can still take showers?"

Brice stood and followed her inside. "I know I'm thankful for it, along with the generator they have for the well. Otherwise, this place would soon develop quite a smell."

As they walked through the lodge toward the staircase, Misty could hear Frankie and Merrick talking from the back room. She couldn't hear what they were saying, but by the tone in their voices, it was obvious the conversation wasn't a pleasant one.

"Sometimes I'm really glad I don't have any siblings," Brice muttered under his breath as they climbed the stairs.

Misty chuckled. "I always wanted siblings, but I'm beginning to think it's not always what it's summed up to be."

"I think it also has to do with one's personality," Brice stated as he stopped at his bedroom door. "Mrs. Frankie seems mighty difficult and moody."

"I can't disagree with you on that one," Misty replied. Touching his arm, she smiled and said, "Good night, Brice. I'll see you in the morning."

CHAPTER 22

With the dawning of Wednesday morning, cell phone service was finally back in working order. Everyone was allowed to take turns charging their phones on the generators, and as soon as Misty and Brice had enough juice, they texted his family through the group chat. Thankfully, the message seemed to go through, and within seconds, their phones were blowing up with replies.

"Officer Mitchell told us someone was killed up there, and we have been worried sick!" Mrs. Amy texted.

"Thank God y'all are okay!" Tori wrote. She then added, *"Although he misses you like crazy, Misty, Wally is doing great."*

Pops sent several excited acronyms and emojis, which made Misty laugh. "Look at him, acting like a young person," she told Brice.

"When are y'all coming home?" Mr. Neil wanted to know.

"Not sure yet," Brice told them. *"We have to wait until the sheriff gets here and says we're free to leave."*

"I hate it that you'll have to be away from the store for so long," Misty said to Brice.

"Pops can manage without me for a few more days," Brice replied. "Uncle Neil will probably help out, too, if Pops needs him."

"Are y'all sure this guy's death was an accident?"

The text was from Tori, and the rest of the family quickly chimed in.

"Tori, the man fell and hit his head," Mr. Neil wrote.

"Yeah, but was he old and feeble? I've fallen before, too, but never died while doing it."

"He wasn't old and feeble," Misty told them.

"What was he like?" Tori asked. *"Did he seem likable, or like the sort of man who would have enemies?"*

"He definitely had enemies," Misty replied. *"No one wanted him here."*

"If there's a killer up there, y'all please be careful!" Mrs. Amy wrote.

"You know," Misty said to Brice as she put her phone down, "since it's going to be a while before the police can get here, why don't we do a bit more investigating ourselves?"

Giving her a look, Brice said, "I thought we already did that when you snuck into Terrence's room. What exactly do you have in mind now?"

"Something very safe and innocent," she replied, holding up her phone. "Social media. Why don't we poke around and see what we can find online?"

After grabbing a snack downstairs, Misty and Brice went back to her room and began looking everyone up on their social media pages. Neither Merrick nor Hudson had accounts, but everyone else did. Frankie's, however, wasn't public, so all Misty could see was who she was connected with.

"It looks like she's connected with Evelyn and Caleb, but not with Terrence," Misty told Brice.

"Listen to this," Brice said. "Caleb isn't connected with Terrence, but his wife is."

"Really?" Misty quickly searched for Evelyn and clicked on her page. "Terrence also liked nearly all of her posts," she stated. "Including the post where Evelyn said she and Caleb were coming to the lodge's anniversary festival."

Misty continued to scroll through Evelyn's account, looking at her photos and reading the comments. There were a few pictures of their daughter, a poodle named Curly, and Evelyn's new car, which was parked in front of a nice house. Misty noticed, however, that although the house was nice, it wasn't a mansion in Nob Hill, which confirmed Misty's suspicion that Caleb didn't make as much as Evelyn tried to act.

"Hey, look, here's a picture of Frankie," Misty said, showing it to Brice.

The caption read, "Girl trip time!" but Misty noticed Frankie didn't look very excited to be going on the trip. When she pointed it out to Brice, he stated drolly, "Does Frankie *ever* look excited? I don't know how she and Evelyn have stayed friends all these years.”

Misty agreed and was searching through more of the girl trip photos when she noticed something. She tapped one of the pictures and drew it in closer, her mind trying to make sense of it all. Taking a screenshot of the picture, Misty decided to give it some more thought before saying anything to Brice.

“That’s strange,” Brice suddenly muttered, and Misty glanced over his shoulder to see what he’d found. Her eyes widened in surprise when she saw that Luke and Terrence were connected, as Luke had consistently denied knowing the man.

“Why do you think they’re connected?” she asked Brice. “Luke said he didn’t know Terrence.”

Brice shook his head and sighed. “I don’t know, but I intend to ask him about it.”

“Was there anything suspicious on Caleb’s page?” Misty wanted to know.

“Not really,” Brice replied. “He doesn’t post much. There were a few pictures of their daughter and some of his coworkers. His social media presence is about the same as he is in person; quiet and subdued.”

“Well, it’s about time for supper, so let’s head downstairs and see if we can do some poking around there,” Misty said, locking her phone.

“Right.” Brice saluted. “I’ll see what I can get out of Luke.”

After grabbing a sweater, Misty followed Brice downstairs, her nose sensing the aroma of grilled chicken floating in the air. When they arrived in the candlelit dining room, everyone was already there mingling and chatting as they waited for Delta to bring in the food.

"Smells delicious, doesn't it?" Misty asked Evelyn, who just happened to be standing by herself, sipping on a glass of sweet tea.

"Yes, it certainly does," Evelyn replied with a smile. She was wearing a very attractive red dress and her hair was pulled into a French twist, showing off a glittering pair of diamond earrings. How the woman managed to look so put together by the light of a lantern or candle was beyond Misty.

"It's a shame you and Frankie didn't get to go on your shopping trip this week," Misty commented.

"Oh, we'll go another time," Evelyn replied, waving a hand in the air. "We try to take at least two girl trips a year; we always have so much fun."

"Y'all certainly have stayed close all these years," Misty stated, her eyes following Brice as he approached Luke. "Where did you say you and your husband live now?"

"Asheville," Evelyn replied. "That's where Caleb is from."

"He's an accountant, right?"

Turning to look at Misty with a flash of surprise lighting her blue eyes, Evelyn said, "Yes, he is. How did you know that?"

"I believe Merrick mentioned it," Misty replied, innocently. Glancing at Evelyn's earrings, she said, "By the way, those earrings are lovely. They look very…luxurious."

Clearing her throat, Evelyn said, "Oh, thank you. My, uh, sister gave them to me for my fiftieth birthday. If you'll excuse me now, Misty, I believe my husband just motioned for me to join him."

Knowing full well her husband had done no such thing, Misty watched as Evelyn hurried away. It seemed she'd hit a nerve when mentioning the obviously expensive jewelry in the same sentence as Caleb's job. Evelyn knew Misty suspected something and was getting nervous. Were Misty's suspicions correct, though? She couldn't be certain, nor did she know just yet how to prove it.

"How did it go?" she asked Brice when he joined her moments later.

"Luke said he connected with Terrence after they met this weekend," Brice replied, keeping his voice low. "Something about Terrence wanting to hire Luke to do some computer work for him."

"Do you think that's true?" Misty asked.

Brice shrugged. "I wouldn't have doubted it before, but now I'm not sure about anything."

"I know what you mean," Misty muttered.

Delta entered just then from the back deck with a cart full of food, interrupting their conversation. As everyone prepared to eat the delicious meal, Misty slowly glanced around the room, wondering if a murderer truly was in their midst. If so, who?

CHAPTER 23

Tori

Wednesday evening, Tori went to the police station again for another self-defense lesson. She came prepared this time with the appropriate clothes, and as they practiced the first move Dylan had taught her the night before, she was pleased with how much faster she was this time.

"You're a natural," Dylan told her. "Ready to try a new one? It's not as hard, I promise."

Nodding eagerly, Tori said, "Let's do it."

"Okay, so one of the major targets predators go for is the neck," Dylan said. "Wrap your hands around my neck and I'll show you how it's done."

Doing what he said, Tori blinked in surprise when he quickly ducked under her arms and out of her grasp.

"A man is usually going to be stronger than a woman," Dylan said, "so instead of putting your arms between your attacker's and trying to force them to let go, simply step back and duck underneath their grasp. Want to try it now that you've seen how it works?"

Tori nodded, and when Dylan came toward her

with his hands outstretched, he told her to tighten her neck muscles. "This is one time you'll want to have a double chin," he said, and Tori did as he instructed. When his hands wrapped firmly around her throat, she stepped back and bent, but didn't go low enough. Instead, she simply banged her forehead on his wrist.

"Try again, but make sure you duck far enough down so that doesn't happen," Dylan said. "Once you're out, that's when you'll make a run for it."

Tori tried again, and this time was successful. She turned to run but stopped short when Dylan grabbed her ponytail. Going off of instinct, she tried to pull away, only causing him to pull her hair harder.

"Stop fighting and twist around to the outside, go underneath my arm, and face me." She did as he said, but he still had a hold of her hair. "Now quickly grab my head and pull it down, either striking my face or my groin with your knee."

Tori hesitated, afraid she might hurt him. When she glanced at him questioningly, he added with a small smile, "Don't do it too hard, though."

Making certain to be gentle, Tori grabbed his head and pulled it downward, while raising her knee at the same time. She felt his face touch her knee, and they both let go and stepped back.

"Good job," he said, giving her a high five. "Just keep in mind that you have to move fast. Your main goal is to catch your attacker off guard, and once he's down, get out of there."

Tori nodded. "I'll try," she said. "Although, I hope I never have the opportunity to use any of these moves."

"I agree," Dylan replied. Hesitating, he looked at her uncertainly and asked, "I didn't hurt you when I grabbed your hair, did I?"

"No," Tori assured him, shaking her head. "Taking me by surprise is a good thing; it will help me be more prepared."

"Good." Dylan smiled in relief. After taking a swig of water, he added, "Let's practice a bit more before we finish up tonight."

They practiced for another thirty minutes, and once they were finished, Tori was feeling more confident.

"I'm really beginning to think I can actually defend myself if ever I need to," she said.

"Good," Dylan replied with an encouraging smile. "I don't think you're quite ready for a black belt, though. Let's keep practicing for another couple of weeks, and it wouldn't hurt for you to come in monthly to keep it fresh in your mind."

"This is really nice of you, Dylan," she told him as she grabbed her regular clothes to go change into. "Look, as a way to sort of pay you back, why don't I buy you supper at Mr. Donovan's place sometime?"

As soon as the words left her mouth, Tori felt her cheeks immediately flush. Had she just asked him out? Her face burning, she opened her mouth to retract the invitation, or at least make it sound like something other than a date, but she was too late. He was already nodding his head in acceptance.

"That sounds great, and I actually haven't had supper yet. Want to go now? I'm off duty."

Attempting to act anything but extremely embarrassed, Tori smiled tightly and stammered, "Y-yes, I'm, uh, also hungry. Just give me a minute to change."

After changing her clothes, Tori quickly touched up her hair and hurried back out to meet Dylan. He'd changed out of his uniform and was waiting patiently for her, and with a smile, she followed him out to their cars.

As Tori drove, she called her mom to tell her about the date…or not date…or whatever this was.

"It's just supper with a friend," she told her. "I only hope he doesn't think I'm trying to hit on him."

"I doubt he thought that, honey," Amy said, and Tori could hear the smile in her voice. "Have fun. Your dad and I are going over to the church in a little while for a dinner they're holding for our age group."

"You mean the senior citizens?" Tori teased.

"You know good and well we're not *that* old yet, young lady," her mom stated with a laugh. "Oh, Wally's had his supper, by the way, so there's no need to worry about him."

"Thanks, Mom. I'll see y'all later," Tori said before disconnecting the call.

When Tori and Dylan walked into *Pat's Kitchen,*

Mr. Donovan was just coming out of his office. When he spotted them, his eyes lit with pleasure.

"It's so nice to see you two," he greeted them. Looking at Tori, he asked, "Have you heard from Brice and Misty?"

"Yes, they texted us today," Tori told him, and his face filled with relief.

"Thank God they're okay," he said. Directing them toward a table, he said, "I'll be leaving for that dinner at the church in about thirty minutes, but let me know if y'all need anything, okay?"

Tori thanked him, and after he walked away, she glanced around the large room to find that she knew almost everyone there. The town's local author, Jeremy Neely, was there with his mother, as well as Adam Dawson's parents, Ambrose and Eloise. When Tori spotted Adam sitting next to his father, her eyes widened in surprise. He'd told Misty he was going to be in North Carolina for a few weeks, so what was he doing here now?

As if feeling her eyes boring into him, Adam glanced over his shoulder and spotted Tori. His handsome face immediately brightened with pleasure, and he stood up to come speak to her.

"Hey, Tori," he greeted her, as pleasant as always. Clapping Dylan on the shoulder, he said, "Dylan, how's it going?"

"I'm good, thanks," Dylan replied.

When Adam looked at Tori again, she inwardly begged, ***"Don't ask about Misty, don't ask about Misty."***

"Tori, I'm surprised to see you tonight; Misty told me y'all were still in Dahlonega," Adam said, and she tried to cover the groan that passed her lips by coughing into her napkin. "I texted her this afternoon, and she told me she was stuck there because of an accident or something. Did y'all just get home?"

"Uh, no, she's still there," Tori stammered. She knew Misty hadn't told him that Brice was with her, so how was Tori supposed to avoid spilling the beans?

"Oh, did y'all drive separately?"

Tori could feel Dylan's eyes boring into her and knew he was wondering why she suddenly seemed so nervous. With a sigh, she looked up at Adam and said, "I didn't go to Dahlonega with her. My shop oven stopped working at the last minute, and I wasn't able to go."

His brow wrinkling in confusion, Adam asked, "Who is with her then?"

"Well, since I couldn't go, Brice decided to just take the extra room we'd already paid for," Tori rambled, her mind whirling. Misty was going to kill her. "He has a friend there from college, you know, so he was happy to have the chance to go see him."

Adam blinked and stared at her for a moment without saying a word. Tori twisted and fidgeted in her seat, glancing at Dylan to find him looking between them curiously.

"Brice went with her?"

Tori couldn't tell by the tone in his voice if Adam was angry or simply hurt. When he stuffed his hands into his pockets and glanced down at the ground, however, she felt horrible for being the one to tell him.

"Yes, Brice is with her," Tori replied, her voice strained.

Before she could think of a way to smooth it over or even change the subject, Adam forced a smile and said, "Well, I'll let the two of you get back to your dinner. See y'all around."

When he walked off and rejoined his parents, Dylan muttered, "That was awkward."

Tori sighed and rubbed her eyes. "Tell me about it," she moaned. "He and Misty were just starting to date when she found out Karson Himmel really wasn't her father. She was so blindsided and upset about the whole thing that she sort of just put their relationship on hold. They decided to be friends until she could sort things out, but I know Adam thinks she's dating Brice now. Did you see the look on his face? I think he really cares about her."

"Oh, yeah, there's no doubt about that," Dylan replied. "But how does Misty feel about him? Does she have a thing for Brice?"

Tori shrugged. "Who knows with her? I don't think even *she* knows."

Their food arrived just then, and Tori was about to ask Dylan about his family and where he was originally from when Patrick Donovan suddenly came rushing toward their table, his face ashen.

"Tori," he said in a strangled tone, "I just received a phone call. Your parents have been in a bad accident."

CHAPTER 24

Misty

After supper, Misty went back to her room to do a bit more snooping on Terrence's social media page. When she began going through some of his older photos, she found a few that included his ex-wife. Clicking on the linked name, Misty was immediately taken to Amelia Levine's page. Much to her surprise, she saw that the latest post that Amelia shared was about Terrence's death. Had Merrick or someone contacted her already?

"Just got the news that my gambling, cheating ex-husband was killed in an accident," the post read. *"I don't have all the details yet, but who is ready to celebrate with me?"*

Misty's eyes widened at how cold and bitter Terrence's ex-wife sounded. He'd cheated on her? Apparently, he'd also gambled away a lot of their money, which confirmed Misty's suspicions of why he'd come home. She considered messaging Amelia and asking who he'd been having an affair with but didn't have the nerve.

With a sigh, Misty closed her phone and went downstairs in search of something to drink. The front desk was empty, so she went into the dining room and got a bottle of water they kept out for the guests. She then decided to go outside and take a walk. After reading Amelia's post, she felt that the fresh air and a bit of exercise would do her good.

The air was cool and the night dark, and Misty reached into her pocket for the flashlight Merrick had given her. She walked slowly, the small beam bouncing along the ground as the chorus of what sounded like a million crickets filled the silence. She was so engrossed in her thoughts that she didn't realize how far she'd strayed from the lodge, and when she looked up, she realized she'd almost reached the trails.

Suddenly, the sound of rustling leaves split the night air, and the chirping of the crickets came to a halt. Misty stopped dead in her tracks as she pointed her flashlight in the direction of the sound, her eyes fervently searching the shadows. In just a matter of seconds, her flashlight found its target. About thirty yards down the trail, two golden eyes appeared in the darkness, caught in the beam of her light. They peered back at her with an eerie calm, totally unmoving except for a continuous, slow blinking. It felt strange that she couldn't see the creature's head or the rest of its body, only those glowing, blinking eyes, and an odd chill crept up her spine. Slowly, she began to back away, her gaze never leaving the creature.

Just then, the eyes began to sway back and forth and point down toward the ground. Sensing that it might charge at her, Misty spun on her heel and hurried back toward the lodge. She glanced over her shoulder to see if it followed, but the shadows were too heavy to find any movement. When she reached the back porch, she held tightly to the banister and pointed her flashlight out into the yard. The beam touched upon bushes, grass, and trees, but this time, the blinking golden eyes were gone.

It was nearly midnight, and everyone was in bed. Dressed all in black, Misty quietly snuck out of her room and down the hallway, bobby pin in hand. She wanted to look at Terrence's room once more; she hadn't had the opportunity to be very thorough the first time.

The large house was dark and quiet, and when Misty reached Terrence's door, she gently pushed the bobby pin into the lock and twisted. When it popped open, she shoved the hairpin into her pocket and quickly stepped inside the dark room, closing the door behind her. She slid her hands into Brice's work gloves and shone her flashlight around the room, shivering at the speck of blood that still glimmered from the side table. In the dead of night, the room felt almost like a tomb, and Misty had to force her legs to move forward as she began her search.

She peered under the bed, side tables, and chest

of drawers. She then looked inside the closet, the bare clothes hangers casting shadows along the back of the wall as she looked around the small space. Nothing. With a sigh, she turned and headed for the bathroom, stopping when she realized Terrence's suitcase was lying open. She'd closed it before, hadn't she? Stepping closer, she peered inside, her eyes widening as her gaze reached the mesh pocket. Unzipping it for a closer look, her suspicions were confirmed: the manila envelope with the photos was gone. Misty carefully searched the rest of the suitcase, but the envelope was nowhere to be found. Someone had come into the room after Misty's first visit and stolen the pictures.

Misty was about to close the suitcase and continue searching the room when she spotted something that looked a bit unusual. Terrence's toothbrush holder was inside the suitcase instead of in the bathroom, and she noticed it appeared longer than the average toothbrush. Carefully pulling it open, she looked inside to find that it was empty, but there seemed to be an extra little compartment at the bottom. After jiggling and twisting it a few times, it finally came off, and a small flash drive tumbled out.

Misty stared down at the device for a moment, wondering what could be on the flash drive that Terrence so obviously wanted to keep it hidden. In her search of the room, she hadn't seen a laptop, but Brice had brought his along. Did she dare take the flash drive and see what was on it?

Swallowing her nerves, Misty quickly shoved the device into her pocket, hoping she wouldn't come to regret that decision. As soon as she took a look inside the flash drive, she'd replace it.

Taking a deep breath, Misty continued on into the bathroom, her soft-soled slippers tapping lightly against the bathroom tile as she carefully looked around. She checked under and around the sink, in the bathtub, and even behind the toilet. She then opened the linen closet and peered inside, shining the flashlight all along the towels and washcloths. She kneeled down and looked inside the little toiletry baskets on the floor of the closet, not finding a thing. Something caught her eye, however, as she was about to stand up and close the door. Resting behind the shadow of one basket was a small turquoise bead. Misty gently retrieved the familiar-looking piece and studied it for a moment, wondering exactly where she'd seen it before. Due to a large amount of Native American décor in the lodge, there were many beads like this around, but she'd seen this one in particular before; she just couldn't remember where.

Standing to her feet, Misty took a closer look at the bead, her eyes widening at what appeared to be tiny specs of blood dotting the outside. If the blood was Terrence's, how did the bead end up at the bottom of the linen closet?

Misty stood there for a moment, pondering what to do. Should she put the bead back and hope the police found it? What if the person who took the photos came back, found the bead, and destroyed it?

Deciding to take the bead with her for safekeeping, Misty carefully placed it inside a small plastic bag and put it into her pocket with the flash drive.

Time to get out of here, she told herself as she closed the door to the linen closet and left the bathroom.

She'd made it halfway across the room when a creak sounded out in the hallway, and she froze. Quickly covering the flashlight beam with her hand, she listened, immediately recognizing the soft sound of footsteps as they walked down the hall in her direction. Heart in her throat, Misty hurried the rest of the way across the room and quickly but gently turned the lock on the door. She then backed away and waited, her eyes glued to the doorknob.

Then, just as she'd expected, the doorknob began to turn. Would they do as Misty had done and pick the lock? She considered throwing the door open and confronting whoever it was, but what then? They could kill her before she could awaken the others, and if they didn't, everyone would then wonder why she was poking around in Terrence's room. She wasn't certain what to do, but knew that now wasn't the time to initiate any confrontations.

Her heart pounding, Misty kept her flashlight

beam covered and waited. The knob jiggled a few times, and then there was complete silence. After a moment, the sound of retreating footsteps reached Misty's ears, and she breathed a sigh of relief.

After waiting for a few minutes, Misty left Terrence's room. She locked the door, closed it quietly behind her, and then hurried back to her own room. She took the plastic bag and flash drive from her pocket and put them somewhere safe; she didn't want them to disappear like the manila envelope. She then made certain that her bedroom door was locked and went to bed, eager to use Brice's computer in the morning.

CHAPTER 25

Tori

The blood left Tori's face as she stared at Mr. Donovan in shock. Her parents had been in an accident? What sort of accident? Her world tilted for a moment, and from what sounded like a million miles away, she heard herself ask, "Wha-what? What do you mean?"

"I don't exactly know what happened," Mr. Donovan said as he wrung his hands anxiously. "One officer that responded to the scene has been trying to reach you but said you weren't answering your phone. Since your mom knew you were here, she told him to call me."

Tori immediately grabbed her purse and searched for her phone. When she couldn't find it, she realized with a sinking stomach that she'd accidentally left it in the car.

"Her mother is okay then?" Dylan asked, already on his feet.

"I believe so, but I don't know for certain." With worry-filled eyes, Mr. Donovan looked at Tori and added, "They're taking your father to Savannah; they just left in the ambulance."

A flood of emotions, including panic, began

pouring over Tori as tears immediately sprung into her eyes. She slowly pushed herself to her feet, her entire body shaking.

"Come on, I'll drive you," Dylan said, gently taking her arm.

Tori let him lead her outside and then stopped at her car to grab her phone. Her stomach clenched when she saw all the missed calls, and she felt overwhelmed with guilt for not being there when her mother needed her. When they got into Dylan's car, she immediately dialed her mom, but it went straight to voicemail. With a sigh, Tori put her phone into her purse.

"No answer," she told Dylan, her voice heavy. "Her phone must have been damaged in the accident."

Without saying a word, Dylan reached across the console and took her hand. Clutching his fingers, Tori stared out the window, seeing nothing. Her mind was filled with worry and despair and thoughts of "what if". What if her parents weren't alright? What would she do without them? They were her rock in this world; they meant everything to her.

Trying to calm herself, Tori leaned her head back against the seat and closed her eyes. Hot tears made their way past her eyelids and down her cheeks, and her lips moved in a silent prayer. She prayed for her parents, and also for strength. If the news really was bad for either of her parents, she would need to be strong.

When they arrived at the hospital, Dylan let Tori out at the emergency room entrance while he went in search of a parking spot. On trembling legs, Tori went inside, her eyes desperately searching the faces. When she spotted Amy, Tori's heart leaped in her chest and she quickly rushed to her mother's side.

"Oh, Mama, are you okay?" she asked, gently pulling her mother into an embrace. Amy's face was covered in scratches and a large bruise was already forming on her arm, but she otherwise seemed okay.

After a moment, Amy pulled back and wiped her eyes. "Yes, I'm fine," she said, nodding. "I just have a few cuts and bruises. I don't know about your father yet, though. The doctor is evaluating him now."

"What happened?" Tori wanted to know, as they found a couple of seats to themselves.

Amy sighed. "From what I could tell in all the chaos, one of the truck's tires came off."

Tori's eyes widened. "What on earth could have caused that?"

"I don't know, but we were driving to the church and everything seemed fine when all of the sudden the truck tilted. Before your father could react, we veered off the road and flipped into the ditch." Amy's eyes filled with tears and she added in a choked voice, "All I remember is hearing a horrible crash and then waking up to hear your father moaning. Tori, his leg was so mangled that

I could see the bone sticking out. By the time the ambulance arrived, he was almost delirious from the pain and loss of blood. I've never been more terrified in all my life."

Tori felt her face turn white as her mother described her father's condition. Her heart clenching, she pulled Amy into another hug and whispered, "I'm scared, too, Mom. At least we've got each other."

Dylan entered the room then with Pops following close behind. His eyes were filled with worry for his son, and Tori waved to them from across the room.

"Have you heard anything yet?" Pops asked as he sat down, his voice trembling.

"No," Amy replied, reaching out to squeeze her father-in-law's hand.

"Should we call Brice and Misty?" Tori questioned.

"I don't want them driving here tonight," Amy stated. "It's dangerous enough to drive at night, but knowing how upset Brice will be will just make it worse. We'll call them first thing in the morning."

Dylan took the seat next to Tori's, and they all waited for another thirty minutes before the doctor finally came out to give them an update on Neil. Tori's heart pounded as she watched him head their way, his face tight. What would they do if the news was bad?

Taking a seat beside Amy, the doctor said, "Mrs.

Barlow, your husband is being prepared for surgery as we speak. I believe he's going to be okay, but his leg is severely broken and he's lost a lot of blood; he also has a couple of cracked ribs. The surgery should take around two hours, but it may be longer with the shape his leg is in." Pausing, the doctor took off his glasses and rubbed his eyes. He then replaced the glasses and looked at Amy in a very serious, straightforward manner as he continued. "I'd be lying to you if I said his leg can positively be saved. At this point, I can't be certain, but I promise to do my best."

Nodding solemnly, Amy said in a hoarse tone, "I understand. Thank you, Doctor."

The doctor patted her hand, nodded to the rest of the family, and then hurried from the room. Tori watched him go, her heart heavy. Surgery was always a serious thing, and knowing that her father may lose his leg made her feel sick to her stomach. How would he handle such news? He was such a strong, energetic man who loved tending to the ranch and his horses. What would it do to him to lose a leg?

Just then, Mr. Donovan and Pastor Alvin stepped into the room. When they spotted the Barlows, they hurried to their side.

"After Tori left, I called Pastor Alvin and told him what happened," Mr. Donovan said. "Are you okay, Amy? How is Neil?"

The two men sat down as Amy explained everything the doctor just told them, and once she was finished, Pastor Alvin took their hands and they all began to pray. Tori cried as they asked God for help, her spirit in anguish over what was happening.

Once they'd finished praying, Dylan went outside to make a phone call, and Tori did her best to try to relax. She'd just picked up a magazine and was mindlessly flipping through its pages when she spotted Dylan beckoning for her to join him outside. Excusing herself, she stood up and hurried out into the cool night air.

"Is something wrong?" she asked him.

"I know you have a lot on your plate right now," he said, his jaw tense, "but I thought you should know something. I called Sheriff Ward back in Shady Pines, and he said that the officer who responded to the accident isn't convinced it was really an accident, after all."

Her eyes widening, Tori asked, "What do you mean?"

"After the ambulance left with your parents, he took a closer look at the tire that came off. He thinks the lug nuts may have been purposefully loosened."

Tori stood there in shock as everything Dylan just said sank in. "Julian Cooper?" she asked after a stunned silence.

"I don't know," he replied with a sigh, "but you need to be extra careful, Tori. This man could be anywhere."

CHAPTER 26

Tori

The next two hours passed by with agonizing slowness. As each minute ticked by on the clock, Tori felt she was living a year within those sixty seconds. When the next hour passed and there was still no word on her father, Tori went down the hall to get something from the drink machine.

As she walked, Dylan's words about her parents' accident echoed through her mind, and she suddenly felt a darkness looming over her. She looked closely at every person she passed, fearing that one of them might be Julian Cooper. Could he be here at the hospital, waiting for the chance to get her alone? Or was Dylan wrong and her parents' tire coming off truly was an accident? If it wasn't, that meant *she* was responsible. If her father lost his leg, it would be *her* fault.

With trembling fingers, Tori bought the drink and spun around to head back to the emergency room waiting area. What she hadn't realized was someone had been following her, and when she nearly smashed into the man standing behind her, she jumped back with a gasp.

"Whoa, are you okay?"

Staring up at Dylan, Tori placed a hand on her chest and nodded. "Yes," she replied breathlessly. "You just startled me, that's all."

"I'm sorry," he said with a sheepish smile. "I just thought you shouldn't be out here by yourself."

The two headed back to rejoin the others, and after drinking her Sprite, Tori got up to pace around the room. Pops joined her, and the two began to share fond memories of Neil. Pops told stories that Tori had never heard before about her father when he was a boy, and she looped her arm through his as she listened, finding comfort in the sound of his voice.

Finally, a little before midnight, the doctor made an appearance. Tori stood frozen for a moment, almost afraid to hear what he had to say. Had her father made it through the surgery okay? If so, did he still have his leg? Gathering her courage, she hurried over to sit next to her mother as the doctor began to give an update.

"The surgery went better than expected," he said in a tired voice. "He's got a long road of recovery ahead of him, but he's going to be just fine."

"You were able to save his leg?" Tori asked, almost afraid to hope.

"Yes, I was," he replied with a nod. "He may have a slight limp, but hopefully with physical therapy, it won't be very noticeable."

Looking at each other with smiles of relief, Amy, Tori, and Pops all threw their arms around each other in a moment of thankfulness and celebration. Amy then turned back to the doctor and thanked him profusely.

"We appreciate all you've done, Doctor," she said, tears in her eyes.

"When can we see him?" Pops wanted to know.

"As soon as he wakes up, which should be within the next hour or so," the doctor replied. "The nurse will let you know when that is. Just keep in mind that he'll be very groggy and sleepy, but that's normal."

As she watched the doctor walk away, Tori felt the heavy fog of fear and worry beginning to lift. Tears of joy over the good news slipped down her cheeks, and she hugged her mother once again.

"Thank you for your support and prayers," Amy told Pastor Alvin and Mr. Donovan just before they left.

"Let me know if you need anything," Pastor Alvin said. "You know you can call me night or day."

Tori hugged and thanked both men, and then turned to Dylan. "You should go home, too. You have to work tomorrow, and I don't want you to be so exhausted that you can't do your job."

Keeping his voice low, he asked, "Are you sure you're okay for me to leave with…you know, our suspicions?"

Tori nodded. "Yes, don't worry about me. Go home and get some rest."

"Okay, well, you have my number if you need

anything," he said. "Good night, Tori. I'm so glad your father is going to be okay."

As he turned to leave, Tori called out, "Dylan?" When he turned back to look at her questioningly, she said, "Thank you. For everything."

"You're welcome," he replied, waving goodbye.

Tori waved in return and watched him leave, feeling a bit like their safety was going with him. Julian Cooper wouldn't possibly try anything in the hospital, though, right? Rubbing her arms, Tori warded off the sudden chill of uncertainty that swept over her and took her seat next to her mother. She considered telling Amy and Pops about Dylan's suspicions, but at the look of weariness on both of their faces, she decided to wait.

Nearly two hours passed when the nurse finally came to get them, and Tori, Amy, and Pops followed her to Neil's room.

"He's still not awake," the nurse said, and when she saw the look of concern on everyone's faces, she immediately added, "That sometimes happens, though, when a patient has been through as much as Mr. Barlow. We expect him to be awake by morning."

"Can we stay with him?" Amy asked when they arrived at Neil's room.

"Yes," the nurse replied, nodding. "There isn't a lot of room for three people, but you can all stay if you want."

Tori's heart felt heavy as they entered the room

and she saw her father lying so still and quiet in the hospital bed. His face was covered in cuts and scratches that had been bandaged, and his leg was elevated and wrapped in a cast. She was beyond grateful that he was alive and going to be okay, but it was still hard to see him so ill.

"We're here, honey," Amy said as she stepped over to her husband's bed and gently touched his arm. "Tori, Pops, and I are all here, so you just rest and get better."

The three of them soon settled in for the night, exhaustion weighing heavily on each of them. They all watched Neil for a bit, hoping he would soon show signs of regaining consciousness, but he simply continued to lie there quietly. None of them spoke the question that rested in the back of their minds: what if, for some reason, he never woke up? The question was like a thick fog that hung in the air, but they all sat quietly, not daring to speak such a thing out loud.

Finally, at almost three in the morning, Tori curled up on the tiny couch next to Pops and drifted off to sleep.

Tori slept deeply, but her dreams were filled with disturbing images that blurred together to create an odd sequence of movie-like scenes. She saw Mr. Donovan's distraught face as he rushed toward her, his voice slow and muddled as he told her about the accident. In a flash, she was running toward the hospital on a dark and densely wooded road, her legs so heavy and weak that she could barely move. Suddenly, she heard a sound from behind, and she turned to see a car bearing down on her, its lights bright and blinding. She tried to run faster, to get away, but she couldn't move. She was frozen in place, and as the car drew closer and closer, she saw a reflection of Julian Cooper's face through the windshield.

Tori's eyes popped open, her heart pounding. She lay there for a moment and slowly blinked her eyes as they tried to come into focus, her mind still fuzzy from the dream. Except for a small light by the sink, the room was dark, and she was having a hard time distinguishing which shadows were human and which were not.

As the cobwebs began to clear in her mind, she realized it wasn't the dream that awakened her. No, she'd heard something. She was still curled up next to Pops on the small sofa, her head lying on the armrest. She didn't move or say anything; she simply sat there, looking around. She saw her father still lying in the hospital bed, the monitor beside him beeping continually. Her mother was asleep in the chair next to him. Everyone was quiet and still, so what had awakened her?

Just then, a large shadow next to the door moved, and with a gasp, Tori sat up straight and grabbed for her cell phone. In her haste, she knocked it from the table and it fell to the floor with a loud clatter. Her mother and Pops both awakened with a grunt, while the shadow threw open the door and rushed from the room. Tori jumped up to follow but was stopped in her tracks when Pops grabbed her arm.

"Tori, what on earth is going on?" He wanted to know. "Is it your father?"

At his words, Amy jumped to her feet and turned on the light, her face ashen as she looked down at her husband.

"No, someone was in here," Tori said as she pulled away from Pops and hurried from the room. She looked up and down the hallway, but no one was there. Suddenly, a figure wearing dark clothes came around the corner, nearly bumping into Tori. With a gasp, Tori jumped back, ready to defend herself.

"Oh! Goodness, hon, you scared the daylights out of me. Is everything okay?"

Trying to catch her breath, Tori nodded to the middle-aged nurse and asked in a trembling voice, "Were you in our room just now?"

The nurse shook her head and said, "No, I'm on my way there now. Why? Did another nurse come in to check on y'all?"

"Someone was in our room and ran out when I woke up," Tori explained.

Frowning, the nurse said, "I haven't seen anyone. Are you sure?"

Before Tori could answer, she heard her mom call out for her. Spinning around, both Tori and the nurse hurried into the room.

"What is it, Mom?" Tori asked breathlessly.

"He just moved his hand," Amy cried as she leaned over her husband.

The nurse immediately took over, pulling out her stethoscope and checking all of his vitals. She'd just finished when he moved his hand again and started trying to moan.

"He's finally waking up," the nurse said, her face breaking into a smile.

Holding on to the hope that her father really was going to be okay, Tori gently touched his arm and said, "Can you hear us, Dad? Mom, Pops, and I are all here with you."

Neil's eyelids moved slightly, and then his eyes slowly opened. He blinked a few times, looking very groggy and confused, but after a moment, he turned his head and looked right at Tori. Recognition passed across his face, and a tiny smile pulled at his lips.

"Hi, Dad," she said, tears filling her eyes. "It's good to have you back with us again."

CHAPTER 27

Misty

Thursday morning, Misty was surprised to find several unread messages in the Barlow group chat. When she opened the chat and began to read, her eyes widened and she quickly jumped out of bed. Throwing on her robe, she hurried across the room to knock on Brice's door.

When he didn't answer, she called out, "Brice?" After waiting for a moment with her ear pressed against the door, she threw on some clothes and hurried downstairs in search of him.

"Good morning, Mrs. Frankie," she greeted her host when she walked into the front room. "Have you seen Brice?"

Nodding toward the front door, Frankie said, "He went outside about ten minutes ago."

Thanking her, Misty walked out onto the large front porch to find Brice talking on the phone. He was just saying goodbye as she closed the door, and when he disconnected the call, Misty asked if everything was okay.

"I called Aunt Amy to get more information about Uncle Neil," he said, sighing as he ran his fingers through his hair. "The reception is so bad here that I wasn't able to get much, but I did manage to hear her say he's doing okay this morning. The doctor wasn't certain he was going to pull through at first, but he's going to be fine."

"Thank God," Misty breathed. "I nearly had a heart attack when I read those messages just now."

"Me, too," Brice replied. "I wish I could be there with them. I hate that we're trapped here."

Patting his arm, Misty said, "Hopefully it won't be much longer."

As they walked around the lodge toward the back porch for breakfast, Misty asked Brice about his computer.

"Do you mind if I borrow it?" she asked.

Looking at her curiously, Brice said, "No, of course not. What do you need it for?"

Misty hesitated. "I, uh, would prefer not to say."

Brice stopped walking and put his hand on Misty's arm, forcing her to stop and look at him. "Misty, what's going on?" He wanted to know.

"I don't want to tell you, Brice, because it could possibly get you into trouble," she said, glancing away to avoid his gaze. "I sort of took something that doesn't belong to me, but after I've used your computer, I'm going to put it back. I promise."

"You *took* something?" Brice asked, his eyes wide.

"Look, the less you know, the better," she stated.

Pursing his lips, Brice said, "Fine. Just promise you'll be careful, okay?"

Misty nodded. "I promise."

After they'd eaten breakfast, Misty took Brice's computer into her room and locked the door. Heeding Brice's warning that his computer didn't have much battery life left, she quickly plugged in the flash drive and opened the only folder it contained.

Misty raised her eyebrows at the large amount of files inside the folder, and she tried to carefully but quickly look at each file name as she scrolled through. Some files were about the divorce, some were bank statements that made it obvious he really did have a problem with gambling, and others were emails to and from his lawyer. Misty was beginning to wonder why he'd hidden the flash drive in the first place when she spotted a video at the very bottom of the list.

Clicking on the video, Misty's mouth dropped open when she recognized the face that popped up on the screen. She quickly took out her phone and recorded the video while she watched, her eyes widening with shock at what the video contained. It was apparent that the person didn't realize they were being recorded; it also appeared they were slightly intoxicated. What they were saying, though, was what shocked Misty the most. She'd started suspecting something along those lines, but hadn't realized it ran so deep.

Brice's computer started alerting that the battery was about to die, but the video wasn't finished yet. Biting her lower lip, Misty tapped her finger nervously against her thigh as she waited. The seconds seemed to tick by slower than normal, and just before the video ended, the screen went black.

With a sigh, Misty stopped the recording on her phone, hoping she hadn't missed anything else too important. After placing the video into a locked file on her phone, Misty unplugged the flash drive and put it back in its safe place. She'd have to make certain to replace it in Terrence's suitcase before the police arrived.

Stepping out onto her balcony, Misty leaned against the railing, her mind filled with a whirlwind of thoughts. What did the bead she'd found in the linen closet have to do with the information she'd just heard on that video? She couldn't quite figure it all out, but could feel the pieces starting to fit together. As soon as she remembered exactly where she'd seen that bead before, she'd know who the murderer was.

When Misty returned Brice's computer to him, he said, "Do I dare ask if you found anything?"

"Oh, I found something alright," she told him. "Just don't ask what it was."

"Great," Brice stated drolly. "Are you going to return whatever it was you took?"

"I will later," she replied with a coy smile.

Shaking his head, Brice pulled a map from his back pocket and said, "Mr. Hudson told me there's a beautiful waterfall down one of the trails. He gave me this map earlier and said it's about a couple of miles from here. Want to go searching for waterfalls?"

"Do we dare brave those trails again?" Misty laughed.

"I'm game if you are," Brice replied, winking.

"Sounds good to me. Do you think the trails are clear enough?" Misty asked.

Brice shrugged. "If not, we can always turn back. I just need to get out of here for a while and get some fresh air."

Misty agreed, and after changing her shoes and grabbing a lightweight jacket, she followed Brice downstairs. They looked for Luke to ask if he'd like to join them, but he was nowhere to be found. So, after packing themselves a picnic lunch with Delta's help, the two told Frankie where they were going and headed into the great outdoors.

They'd barely made it down the back porch steps when they suddenly heard the sound of heated voices coming from around the corner of the lodge. Glancing over at Brice, Misty put her finger to her lips and the two slipped quietly in the direction of the voices. Peeking around the corner, Misty spotted Merrick and Hudson standing by themselves beneath a pecan tree. Merrick was saying something to Hudson in a low tone, but Misty could tell the conversation was an unpleasant one just by watching their body language. Merrick was tense as he spoke, pointing his finger at Hudson, and then back at the lodge.

Hudson's face was red and his eyes were angry as he glared at his brother-in-law, his jaw clenched.

"Boy, those two don't look happy," Brice whispered. "Can you tell what they're saying?"

Misty shook her head. "No, unfortunately not."

They heard the back door slam just then, and the two quickly hurried away before someone caught them eavesdropping.

"What do you think that was all about?" Misty asked once they were far enough away not to be heard.

"Who knows?" Brice shrugged. "Maybe family problems. I know a little about that."

Glancing up at him, Misty asked, "Your mom?"

Brice nodded. "Yeah. We never really had much of a relationship, and after Dad died, it only grew worse."

Misty was saddened by Brice's words. She'd always longed to know her mother; if she could have just one memory of her, she'd be happy. Here Brice had his mother and could still be making memories with her, but she'd seemingly rejected him and any relationship they might have had.

"Do you talk to her very often?" she asked.

"On birthdays, and occasionally at Christmas," he replied, stuffing his hands into his pockets as they headed down the trail. "And I'm normally the one who makes the calls. She's just not the type of person you can be close to. Her husband is a truck driver, so he's not home very much."

"Have you met him?" Misty asked.

"Yeah, he seemed like a decent fellow," Brice replied. "Nothing like my dad, though."

"What was he like?" Misty asked as she carefully stepped over a fallen branch.

"Calm and easygoing, with a quiet sense of humor," Brice replied with a small smile. "When Mom would get in her moods, he'd take me fishing and tell me all sorts of interesting stories. He was the best."

Misty's heart clenched at the sadness she heard in his voice. "You must miss him very much," she said softly.

Brice sighed. "Yeah. I think of him every day."

They were silent for the rest of the walk, both too engrossed in their thoughts to say much. Brice navigated their way down the trails with his map, and Misty was glad the debris wasn't so thick that they had to turn back. After the drama of the last few days, she felt that seeing a waterfall would do them both some good. The bubbling brook to the left of the trail filled the silence between them, creating a calm, peaceful atmosphere.

"Hey, I think I hear it," Misty said after they'd been walking for a little over thirty minutes.

Peering at the map, Brice pointed to a bend in the trail ahead and said, "According to this, it should be right up there."

When they rounded the corner, Misty spotted the waterfall through the trees and they picked up their pace with excitement. As they drew closer and the trees gradually thinned to form an oval-shaped frame, Misty caught her breath at the beauty before them. Water cascaded gently down the rocks like a long, majestic wedding veil, spreading out into soft folds of white as it fell peacefully into the water below. It wasn't the largest or grandest waterfall she'd ever seen, but it was just as breathtaking in its simplicity.

"This was worth the walk," Misty breathed.

"It certainly was," Brice agreed. Taking her hand, he said, "Come on; let's get closer."

They spent nearly an hour at the waterfall, enjoying the peaceful serenity that one can only find in nature. Birds chirped, the sky was blue, and the sound of the water rushing over the rocks was enough to make even the most distressed spirit feel calm and relaxed.

They sat on the rocks near the water, talking and eating the picnic lunch they'd brought along. After a while, they reluctantly put everything away and decided to head back to the lodge.

"Hey, look at this," Brice suddenly said, pointing to something on the map.

Leaning over his shoulder to have a look, Misty asked, "What is it?"

"There's an X here on the map next to a place called Devil's Cliff," he said. "Wasn't that where that guy was killed? I think I remember the name from that newspaper article you found in Terrence's suitcase."

Misty's eyes widened. "You mean it's not very far from here?"

Brice shook his head. "It looks like it's just a little further up the mountain; maybe a mile or so." Seeing the glint in Misty's eyes, he said, "Uh oh. I shouldn't have pointed that out."

"Why not?" she asked, tilting her head.

"Because I know that look. You want to go up there, don't you?"

Smiling sweetly at him, she said, "I think that's a great idea. Let's go."

With a sigh, Brice gave in and they headed off in the direction of Devil's Cliff. The climb was a bit steeper than Misty had anticipated, and by the time they made it to the top of the cliff, she was out of breath and her legs were trembling.

"Wow, so this is where it all happened," she said as they stared down at the sudden drop-off.

"Why would Jackson have come here in the middle of the night?" Brice asked, his brow wrinkled in confusion. "This drop-off isn't easy to see in broad daylight, much less in the dark."

"It doesn't really make sense, does it?" Misty said. "Someone had to have lured him up here and pushed him off."

"But who?" Brice wanted to know. "And why?"

Misty shook her head and sighed. "I don't know, but I have a feeling the truth will eventually come out."

It was after four o'clock when the two turned to start making their way back to the lodge. Suddenly realizing she'd left her water bottle on a rock at the edge of the cliff, Misty spun around to retrieve it.

Before she knew what was happening, her foot slipped on a pebble and her body was immediately thrown off balance. The whole world seemed to tilt at that moment, sending her spiraling toward the edge of the cliff so quickly and with such force that she barely had time to react. Everything spun madly about, and with her heart in her throat, Misty knew if she didn't do something drastic to catch herself, she was going to fall over the edge of Devil's Cliff.

CHAPTER 28

A strangled scream somehow managed to escape Misty's throat as she catapulted wildly toward the edge of the cliff. Her mind froze and time seemed to stand still as sheer panic clutched at her heart, and in a moment of razor-sharp clarity, she knew she was about to die. She flailed her arms and grasped at anything she could, but nothing held and she felt her legs go over the edge, her feet finding nothing but emptiness. Tears of horror sprang into her eyes and a prayer for help flitted through her mind, but she couldn't say it out loud. She couldn't say or do anything, but desperately try to catch herself.

As her upper body was slammed against the top of the cliff, the breath was knocked from her lungs. Her hands grasped frantically at the dirt and rocks, hoping to find something solid as she continually slid over the edge. Just when she thought all hope was lost, she suddenly felt a large, warm hand grasp hold of her wrist.

"Oh, God," she heard Brice grunt as he fell to the ground just above her head. Her entire body was dangling from the cliff, and when Misty looked down, panic streaked up her spine and she began to kick her legs furiously.

"Stop kicking, Misty," Brice yelled when his grip on her wrist began to slip.

Looking up through half-crazed eyes, Misty saw Brice hanging halfway over the cliff as he struggled to brace himself. At the look of sheer determination and concentration on his face, Misty heard a voice in the back of her mind telling her to calm down, to quit fighting and help him before she caused them both to plummet to their deaths.

"Wha-what can I do?" she asked breathlessly, her entire arm completely numb.

"Do you see that rock just above your head and to your left?"

Misty nodded, her eyes zoning in on the rock.

"Grab it with your other hand," Brice instructed, his tone strained.

Gathering all of her strength, Misty fought against gravity and raised her arm upward toward the rock. It was higher than she'd realized, but after a few tries, she was able to grasp it.

"Now raise your right leg up until you find that little crevice to put your foot into."

Brice's arm was trembling, and his palm was getting sweaty against her skin. Misty knew if she didn't hurry, he wouldn't be able to save her.

Carefully raising her right leg, Misty found the crevice and shoved her foot inside, a moment of relief flooding over her at the feeling of something solid beneath her foot.

"Can you push into the crevice and raise yourself

up a bit?" Brice asked just as a bit of sweat dripped from his chin onto her forehead.

Misty nodded, and gritting her teeth, she pushed against the crevice, hoping it wouldn't give out on her. If it did, the force of her body suddenly dropping several inches would surely rip her wrist from Brice's grasp.

Thankfully, the rocks held, and Misty was able to raise herself up enough for Brice to grab her under the shoulders. She grasped hold of the rocks on either side of him as he took a deep breath and gathered his strength. With a grunt, his arms tensed and he quickly pulled her body up and over the remainder of the cliff in one swift movement.

The two collapsed in a heap on the ground, their chests heaving from the exertion and bodies trembling as the adrenaline slowly began to fade away. After nearly drowning a few months before, Misty thought nothing could ever top that horrible experience. Until now.

"Are you okay?" Brice asked in a hoarse, breathless tone.

"I-I think so," Misty panted. "Are you?"

Brice slowly sat up and nodded. "Yeah, I'm okay," he replied. His shirt was torn and covered in dirt, and Misty spotted specs of blood on his hands and forearms where the rocks had scraped the skin off.

Feeling light-headed, Misty attempted to stand up but quickly found that she couldn't. Her legs were like Jell-O and she felt sick to her stomach.

Sliding far enough away from the edge of the cliff so that falling off was no longer a threat, Misty put her head between her knees.

"Here, drink this," Brice said as he gently handed her a bottle of water.

Misty sipped on the water for a moment, hoping it wouldn't come back up. Having a near-death experience was enough to leave anyone shaken, and Misty could feel every nerve in her body sizzling and throbbing.

"I don't think I can make it back to the lodge, Brice," she stated weakly.

"Don't worry about that right now," he said. "Maybe you'll feel stronger after you've rested for a bit. Do you want to try to eat a little something? Delta sent some trail mix with us."

Misty shook her head. "I don't think I can eat right now."

Reaching out to touch her wrist gently, Brice frowned and said, "Your wrist is starting to swell; I hope I didn't break it."

Misty carefully wiggled her wrist back and forth and said, "I think it's just bruised."

With a sigh, Brice stood and slowly took in their surroundings. After a moment, he looked back at Misty and said, "Well, I guess we'll just have to stay here for the night."

"I might can make it…"

Brice shook his head, interrupting her protest. "No, it's too strenuous of a hike for either one of us after what we've been through. We'll sleep here and hopefully feel well enough in the morning to head back."

"But what about wild animals?" Misty asked with a shiver.

"Hey, I may work at a hardware store, but Pops and my dad made sure I knew how to build a fire," he replied with a wink. "Plus, who knows? Maybe someone from the lodge will come looking for us and we won't have to stay the entire night."

Nodding, Misty agreed and asked Brice to help her up. "I don't want to camp too close to the cliff," she told him.

With his arm around her waist, Brice supported Misty as she stood. Her head began swimming wildly about, and for a moment, she feared she might lose the contents of her stomach.

"Are you okay?" Brice asked with concern.

Misty nodded. "Y-yes, I think so."

As they slowly moved further from the cliff, Misty realized that every muscle and bone in her body ached. She felt as if she'd been run over by a train, and could only imagine how much worse it would be after a few hours. Her clothes were torn and dirty, just like Brice's, and her hands were raw and bloody from grasping at the rocks. Thankfully, she'd had the foresight to bring along her first aid kit, and once they were settled, she intended to use it.

As they went down the hill, Misty glanced back at the cliff, watching as the place where Jackson Dagon had died grew further and further away.

She'd almost died there, too, and wondered if Jackson's death really was an accident after all.

Once they reached a more level area, Brice helped Misty to the ground as he set about building a fire. In just a few moments, a warm, cozy blaze was crackling and popping.

"I'm very impressed by your woodsman skills," she complimented him with a teasing smile.

Brice laughed. "Thanks. Just don't expect me to make a snare and catch our supper."

"Thankfully, we have the trail mix and some water left," Misty said as she dug around the backpack in search of the first aid kit. Once she'd found it, she doctored both of their wounds as best she could.

"I'm shocked that at least one of us didn't break something," Brice stated as Misty slathered salve across his scraped knuckles.

Once she was finished, it was after seven o'clock and the sun was starting its descent. Misty slid into the lightweight jacket she'd brought along and began snacking on the trail mix, her stomach rumbling for supper. The night air was chilly, and she hoped they wouldn't both catch a cold from sleeping outside with no blankets. Looking up at the sky, Misty stared into the darkening abyss and sighed in awe at how many stars filled the heavens.

"What's going on between you and Adam these days?"

Misty quickly moved her gaze downward to look at Brice, feeling surprised by the sudden question.

"Uh, nothing really," she stammered. "We've both been busy and haven't seen much of each other lately."

Brice nodded, his gaze focused on the fire as he poked at it with a stick. "So, you're not dating?"

Misty hesitated, uncertain of how to answer him. Finally, she sighed and said, "No. We decided to just be friends for now until I get everything sorted out."

Brice looked at her then, his gaze intense as he asked, "And when you *do* get it sorted out, then you'll date him?"

"I'm not really sure," she replied. "I guess we'll just have to wait and see."

Brice looked away, but not before Misty saw a flash of…what? Annoyance in his eyes? She couldn't quite tell, but she wasn't about to let him ask about her dating life without answering a few questions himself.

"What about Cassie?" she asked.

Blinking in surprise, Brice's brow lowered and he asked, "What about her?"

"Are you ever going to get over her and move on with your life?"

Brice didn't answer for a moment; he simply stared quietly into the fire, its flames reflecting in his blue gaze. "With nearly every woman in my life, all they've ever done is hurt me," he finally said in a low tone. "It's not that I can't get over Cassie; I wouldn't have her back if she begged me. It's more of an issue with getting over the hurt and trusting someone with my heart again.”

Misty’s chest tightened at his words. She was sorry he’d been hurt by both Cassie and his mom, so badly that he now had a complex about trusting women. In a way, though, she understood. With everything she’d been through in life, trusting people and getting close to them had never come easy for her, either.

“I think I know how you feel,” she said softly. “Even though we can heal and move on from the pain of our past, the scars are still there.”

Brice looked at her then, and something passed between them for the first time. It was a feeling of comfort and familiarity, of two battered hearts finding one another in the dark and knowing they were not only seen but also understood. Misty had always felt a closeness to Brice, but she felt it now more than ever.

“I guess we should probably try to get some sleep, huh?” Brice asked, breaking the silence.

Glancing up at the sky, Misty said, “It’s not even completely dark yet.”

“Yeah, but I’m exhausted.” His eyes glinting mischievously, he added, “Saving a girl’s life wears a guy out.”

Misty laughed. “I’m actually really tired, too. I don’t know if I can sleep on this hard ground, though.”

Tapping his chin, Brice looked around for a moment, his eyes brightening when they landed on the backpack. Pouring its contents out onto the ground, he then filled the bag with leaves and pine straw.

"Your pillow, m'lady," he said as he proudly handed her the bag.

Misty took the bag with a smile. "You are too kind, good sir," she said, her entire body aching as she settled down on the cold, hard earth.

They both lay on either side of the fire, listening to the sound of the brook bubbling below and the crickets chirping from the bushes. Misty shivered and wrapped her arms around her waist as she inched a bit closer to the fire. Brice noticed, and with a concerned frown, he sat up and looked at her.

"Are you cold?" he asked.

"Yes, but I always get cold when it's time to go to sleep," she replied.

He hesitated for a moment, chewing on his bottom lip uncertainly until he finally muttered something under his breath and crawled around the fire to her.

"I'm cold, too," he said. "Would it be awkward if we cuddled?"

"It wouldn't have been if you hadn't used the word 'cuddled'," Misty retorted, rolling her eyes.

Chuckling, Brice stretched out beside her and said, "Sorry. Bad choice of words. Now, give me that comfy pillow I made and you can have my super soft shoulder."

Feeling a little embarrassed, Misty quietly did as he instructed. As soon as she felt the warmth of his body against hers, however, all embarrassment fled and she breathed a sigh of relief. Perhaps now she wouldn't lay out here and freeze to death.

Listening to the steady rhythm of Brice's heart against her ear, Misty closed her eyes and relaxed, knowing she would be safe in his arms.

CHAPTER 29

Tori

After a long day at the hospital, Tori was exhausted. Her father was doing better but was still in a lot of pain, and seeing him hurting so badly broke her heart. Thankfully, their friend and the local veterinarian, Kyra Kirby, went by her parents' house to see about Wally and the horses earlier in the day, but Tori knew she would need to go see about them tonight.

Dylan had called that afternoon to say there was no proof that the lug nuts on her dad's tire had been tampered with. Tori was thankful for that. Perhaps that meant Julian Cooper was long gone and there was no need to worry.

"Pops, can I take your car?" she asked as she gathered her things. "I think I'll just stay at the house tonight and come back up here in the morning."

"I'll drive you," he said. "I need to run by the store and see about a few things, anyway."

Kissing her mom and dad goodbye, Tori promised she'd see them in the morning and followed Pops out to the parking garage. As they drove, Tori's phone vibrated, and she unlocked the screen to see an incoming text from Chris.

"Hey, how are you? Any word on this Cooper fellow?"

She hadn't talked to him since her father's accident, and seeing his name on the screen made her sigh.

"Everything okay?" Pops asked.

Closing her phone, Tori leaned her head back against the seat and said, "Chris Caddel has been texting me since the ordeal with Julian Cooper."

Pops glanced over at her as if trying to gauge her feelings by the expression on her face. "How do you feel about that?" He wanted to know.

Tori shrugged. "It's a little strange, honestly. I haven't heard from him in so long."

"Talking to him brings back a lot of memories, huh?"

"It sure does," she replied softly, looking out the window to watch the sun setting behind the trees.

"You two sure were crazy for one another," Pops stated with a chuckle. "Y'all were a lot like my Nancy and me when we were young."

Turning her head to look at her grandfather, Tori asked, "How did you know Nan was the one?"

Pops smiled, his eyes wrinkling as memories of Tori's sweet grandmother flitted through his mind. "She made me feel complete," he finally said. "I was always very shy, but when I met her, she made me feel so comfortable that I nearly talked her ears off. After that, all I could think of was her. She was one special lady."

Tori nodded in agreement, her heart squeezing with longing for her grandmother and that soft, lavender smell that always seemed to linger on her skin. She and Tori were always so close, and it broke Tori's heart when she was diagnosed with cancer and passed away nearly five years ago.

Reaching across the console, Pops took Tori's hand and gently squeezed it. "You'll know when the time is right, Tori girl. I promise."

Tori patted his hand and smiled at him, grateful for his comforting presence. They talked the rest of the drive to Shady Pines, and when Mr. Donovan's restaurant came into view, she asked him to stop so she could get her car.

"I'm going to pick up Wally and go back to my place for the night," Tori told him.

"Do you want me to stay with you?" Pops asked, his eyes filled with concern, and Tori knew he was still worried about Julian Cooper.

"You can if you want, but I'm sure I'll be fine," Tori told him. "I think Julian Cooper is long gone, but if not, I'll have Wally there to protect me."

Pops nodded. "I'll call you once I'm finished at the store."

Waving goodbye, Tori climbed into her car and headed to her parents' place. Realizing she'd forgotten to answer Chris's text, she decided to just call and give him all the updates.

"Hey, Tori," he answered the phone, a smile in his voice. "How are you?"

"Exhausted," she told him. "My parents were

involved in a really bad car wreck yesterday."

"Oh, no! Are they okay?"

Tori proceeded to fill him in on the details, her eyes so tired and heavy that she could barely focus on the road ahead.

"Wow, I'm so glad they're both okay. The police think it may not have been an accident?" Chris asked once she'd finish.

"That's what they originally thought," Tori said with a nod, even though he couldn't see her, "but after doing a bit more investigating, now they're not so sure. Officer Mitchell told me they can't find any evidence."

"Well, hopefully it wasn't done on purpose," Chris said. "And hopefully this Cooper fellow is long gone."

"I completely agree," Tori replied as she turned down her parents' long dirt driveway.

The sun had completely set now, leaving the sky with just a few lingering shades of periwinkle and dark gray. The wooden fences that lined the ranch were now silhouettes amongst the rolling, green fields, and Tori suddenly had a very clear memory of one summer night many years ago. She and Chris had been dating for a few months, and he'd come over for supper. That night, they'd strolled along those very fences, hand in hand as they talked about their hopes and dreams for the future. It was that night when Chris kissed her for the first time, and she thought her heart was going to beat right out of her chest.

"What was that sigh for?"

Chris's question brought Tori back to the present, and she blinked her eyes, trying to remember what they'd been talking about.

"Sigh?" she asked as she pulled up in front of the house and parked. "What sigh?"

"You sighed just now," he told her.

"Did I? Oh, well, I was just remembering when we…when we were kids."

They really *had* been kids, in a way. It seemed like so long ago when they were together, but at the same time, it seemed almost like yesterday.

"Well, I'd better get off the phone and see about all the animals around here," Tori quickly added before Chris could ask any further questions. "I'll talk to you later, okay?"

"I hope so," he replied warmly.

Saying goodbye, Tori disconnected the call and climbed from the car, feeling much older than her twenty-eight years. With a yawn, she went inside and headed straight for the kitchen, where the loudest bark she'd ever heard echoed off the walls.

"Hey, buddy," she greeted the massive furry beast with the slobbery tongue and wagging tail. "Are you happy to see your Aunt Tori?"

Wally pranced around her legs, begging for back scratches as he gazed up at her with happy eyes. Tori gave him a few quick rubs and then took him outside. While he quickly went about smelling around the yard and do his business, she went into the barn to tend the horses. Trampas, Little Joe,

Marshal Dillon, Heath, and Flint were all happy to see her, along with Kitty, her dad's newest female. She nuzzled each one and gave them a sugar cube along with their supper, and did a quick job of mucking out their stalls. She then cleaned and refilled their water buckets and gave them fresh bedding. Thankfully, Kyra had let them out earlier for some exercise, so with a kiss on each of their noses, Tori said good night and locked up the barn.

"Come on, Wally boy," she called to Misty's dog as she walked back to her car. "You're coming home with me tonight."

The St. Bernard bounded across the yard, quick as a flash, and jumped happily into her back seat. After texting her mom to let her know everything was taken care of at the house, Tori headed home. By the time she pulled into her driveway, it was nearly nine o'clock. She pressed the button to open the garage door, but it wouldn't work. With a sigh, she grabbed her things and told Wally to follow her inside.

"I was wondering if you'd gone out of town."

The voice from across the yard made Tori jump, and she quickly turned to find her new neighbor standing on his front porch, watching her. His name was Hayden Brownley, and he'd moved into the house next to hers last month. He was in his early forties, with thinning brown hair and narrow, mud-brown eyes. He was an odd sort; always hanging around his front yard and asking everyone nosy questions. He, on the other hand, didn't seem to care for anyone to ask *him* questions.

"No, my parents were in a car accident, so I've been at the hospital," she told him, motioning for Wally to sit.

"Are they okay?" he asked, his beady eyes staring at her over the coffee mug he raised to his lips.

Tori nodded. "My dad's leg was broken pretty badly, but it looks like everything is going to be okay."

Hayden didn't immediately respond, and Tori glanced toward her porch, wishing she could just walk inside and not worry about being rude.

"That's good," he finally said.

Forcing a smile, Tori said, "Yes, well, it was good to see you, Hayden. Good night."

Hurrying inside before he could say anything else, Tori closed and locked the door behind her. She then went into the kitchen to fix supper for both Wally and herself.

"That's strange," she muttered to herself when she went to get the mustard for her sandwich out of the cabinet. She normally kept the mustard next to the ketchup and other condiments on the top shelf. This time, however, it was resting on the bottom shelf with the spices.

"I'm losing it, Wally," she told the dog with a chuckle as she grabbed the mustard and began making her sandwich.

A moment later, just as she'd sat down to eat, she realized she hadn't fixed anything to drink. With a sigh, she stood and hurried to the fridge, reaching inside to grab the small pitcher of sweet tea she always kept on the door. When the tea wasn't there, she blinked in surprise and quickly searched the rest of the refrigerator.

"Wow, I really *am* losing it," she muttered under her breath when she spotted the pitcher behind the carton of strawberries on the middle shelf.

Just then, Tori heard something. It wasn't a very loud noise; it was more like a low humming, as if someone stood just outside the kitchen window, humming a tune. An eerie chill crept up her spine, and Tori glanced down at Wally, expecting to see him in defense mode. Instead, he was happily eating his massive bowl of kibble, completely oblivious to any strange sounds.

Tori looked hesitantly at the light switch over by the kitchen door. Dare she turn it off and look out the window? Could her nerves take it if someone really was out there? Taking a deep breath, she gathered her courage and walked toward the light switch. She'd just reached out a trembling hand when her cell phone suddenly rang, echoing loudly throughout the room.

With a gasp, Tori leaned against the wall for a moment as she tried to calm her startled heart. After a couple of breaths, she hurried back to the table and answered the phone.

"I hate to leave you by yourself just yet," Pops said on the other end of the line. "I think I'll come to stay with you tonight if that's okay?"

Feeling a little relieved that she wouldn't be alone tonight, Tori smiled and said, "You know I don't mind. Are you on your way here now?"

"Yep. I'll be there in ten minutes."

When Tori disconnected the call and sat down to eat her sandwich, she realized the humming from outside the back window had stopped.

CHAPTER 30

Misty

Misty opened her eyes, her brain still foggy from sleep. Where was she? She blinked several times, slowly taking in her surroundings. Stars twinkled from the sky above as the moon turned the treetops into silhouettes, and suddenly, she remembered that she and Brice were sleeping near Devil's Cliff.

She sat up and looked around, her ears attuned to the eerie silence that felt so heavy it was almost suffocating. The crickets were no longer singing, and the fire Brice so meticulously built had begun to die, its tiny embers glowing in the night as a heavy chill rested in the air. Shivering, Misty rubbed her arms, wondering what had awakened her. It wasn't until then that she realized Brice was gone.

Suddenly, a rustling sounded from the trees, and when she quickly turned to search the shadows, she gasped. There, only a few feet away, stood a giant black wolf. It stared back at her, its steady gaze glowing in the dark night as the fading light from the fire reflected within the pair of piercing, yellow eyes. It seemed totally undaunted by her presence. In fact, Misty had the feeling it didn't want her there, as if she was trespassing on its territory. It seemed to glare at her with an intense hatred; she could feel it down in her bones.

Her entire body trembling, Misty forced her gaze away from the wild animal and looked frantically around for Brice. Dare she call out to him? They didn't have a gun or any kind of weapon with which to protect themselves. When Misty's eyes landed on the smoldering pile of sticks beside her leg, she carefully reached her hand out to grab one.

Before her fingers could grasp hold of the stick, a low growl broke the silence, and a chill raised the hair on Misty's neck as she spun back around. The wolf was baring its teeth and inching toward her, like a predator stalking its prey. Its yellow eyes and white teeth seemed to glow in the darkness, and before Misty could react, the giant black beast lunged toward her, its paws outstretched and teeth ready to sink into the folds of her neck…

"Misty, wake up!"

At first, Misty struggled against the strong hands that grabbed her arms and shook her. When she heard the familiar voice calling her name, however, something clicked within her brain and she finally began to emerge from the clutches of the nightmare.

Trembling, Misty rapidly blinked her eyes and stared into Brice's face as it came into focus. Her heart was pounding loudly in her chest, and for a moment, she felt like she couldn't breathe.

"Where…where is he?" she gasped, clutching Brice's arm as she frantically jerked her gaze in every direction.

"Who?" Brice wanted to know.

Fighting panic, Misty cried, "The wolf! He was just here…I saw him. Brice, he was going to kill me."

"It was just a dream, Misty," he said, tenderly rubbing her back. "I promise. There is no wolf here."

Still feeling uncertain, Misty looked up at Brice and asked, "Are you sure?"

Brice nodded, his blue eyes soft as he gently brushed her hair away from her face and tucked it behind one ear. They were sitting on the ground, their arms entwined, and something in the way he looked at her made Misty forget all about the bad dream. Their faces were only inches apart, and when Brice's gaze dropped to her lips, Misty found herself leaning toward him.

Perhaps it was the dream that had left her feeling vulnerable, and the comfort of Brice's arms simply made her want to be closer to him. Or perhaps it was something more. Misty couldn't say, but when Brice's lips pressed against hers, the warmth that immediately shot through her veins was so strong, she felt as if she'd been shocked by an electrical current.

Ignoring the voices of caution in her mind, Misty buried her hands in Brice's soft hair, pulling him closer as he wrapped his arms firmly around her waist. The kiss deepened, and the pounding of Misty's heart was so loud that she didn't hear the footsteps as they steadily drew closer.

"Well, boys, it looks like we've been searching for nothing."

With a start, Misty and Brice quickly broke apart and turned to find Merrick, Frankie, and Hudson standing only a few feet away.

"If you were planning to have a lover's getaway and spend the night out here, the least you could have done was tell us," Frankie added in the same snarky tone.

Brice stood with such haste that Misty tumbled over on her backside with a ***harrumph.*** Glancing down at her apologetically, Brice leaned over to help her up.

"We weren't…I mean, this wasn't planned," Brice told them, his cheeks as red as Misty's.

"We were heading back to the lodge when we had an accident," Misty said as she shook the dirt from her clothes. "As you can see from all the cuts and scratches, we were both hurt and unable to make it back to the lodge. We thought we'd just sleep out here tonight and try again in the morning. I can assure you there was nothing more to it than that."

Cocking an eyebrow, Frankie stated drolly, "Yes, we could see that when we arrived."

Misty's face flushed even more, but before she could say anything else in their defense, Merrick shot his sister a dirty look. "That's enough, Frankie," he snapped. "Anyone with eyes can see they're telling the truth." He then hurried to their side, his eyes filled with concern as he asked, "What kind of accident did you have? Are either of you hurt badly?"

"We were up on the cliff when Misty lost her balance and fell over the edge," Brice said. "I managed to grab her and pull her back to safety, but we're both pretty banged up."

"My wrist is swollen, but I don't think it's broken," Misty told Merrick, holding out her arm.

"You both could have been killed," Hudson spoke up, his eyes wide.

"What in the world made y'all come up here in the first place?" Frankie snapped. "Don't you know the cliffs are dangerous?"

"I guess we just weren't thinking clearly," Misty muttered, glancing at Brice with a warning look not to say anything about Jackson Dagon.

"Well, let's get you both back to the lodge," Merrick said.

Rubbing her arms, Frankie glanced around and shivered. "Yes, please," she murmured. "I don't like being up here."

The walk back to the lodge took nearly two hours, and by the time they made it back, Misty was exhausted. Delta was waiting up for them when they arrived, and she insisted Misty and Brice eat something before going to bed.

"That picnic lunch wasn't enough to last you 'til

morning," she said as she quickly fixed them a turkey sandwich.

After eating, Misty and Brice thanked them all for everything. As they headed upstairs, both bleary-eyed and too tired to talk, they said good night and went into their own rooms. All Misty wanted to do was fall into bed and sleep for days, but she forced herself to take a shower and wash her hair first. Once she was finished, it was nearly three in the morning, and her entire body throbbed from exhaustion. She took a Tylenol for the aching in her joints, grabbed her sleep mask, and dove beneath the covers. Within seconds, she was fast asleep.

Misty slept nearly all day Friday. When she finally dragged herself from the bed, she was so sore she could hardly move. After taking another hot shower, she felt a little better and decided to go downstairs in search of something to eat. It was after two o'clock, which meant lunch had already been served, but she hoped Delta would still have something left that she could eat.

"Misty, it's good to see you up," Hudson called from the front room.

Misty was heading for the kitchen, her stomach pinching with hunger, but she turned at the last minute to thank Hudson again for everything they'd done the night before.

"I don't think I've ever been so tired," she told him with a laugh. "I was so relieved to get back to the lodge last night and into that wonderfully soft bed."

"Yes, sleeping on the ground is overrated," he replied with a knowing nod. "I always hated when Frankie and the others wanted to go camping when we were young."

"Why did you go then?" Misty asked, smiling.

"To be with Frankie, of course," he answered with a shrug.

"It seems to have worked for you," Misty stated teasingly.

"Yes, I suppose so," he replied, his tone not very convincing. "Oh, since you hadn't come down yet, you missed the good news at lunch. The sheriff called this morning and said the road coming up the mountain isn't quite as bad as they thought, and he's planning to be here by noon tomorrow."

Misty's eyes widened. "That's wonderful," she exclaimed.

"It certainly is," Hudson replied, nodding. "I know everyone is ready to get back to their normal lives. Evelyn and Caleb said they're quite anxious to go home."

Misty hesitated. "Do you think the sheriff will give the okay for everyone to leave?"

Hudson looked at her curiously. "Why wouldn't he?"

"Oh, well, I wasn't sure if there would be any kind of investigation into Terrence's death," she replied, shrugging nonchalantly.

"I'm sure there will be a standard investigation, but he knows Terrence's death was an accident. I'm sure there will be no problem with everyone going their separate ways," he told her.

Misty nodded. "I see."

Frankie called to him from the back room then, and Hudson excused himself. Misty was just about to turn and head for the kitchen when the cellphone that was lying on the front desk suddenly lit up. Misty wasn't intentionally being nosy; her eyes simply noticed the lighted screen and looked in that direction.

"Whenever you get a chance, we need to talk. I need money ASAP."

Quickly glancing around, Misty grabbed her phone from her pocket and snapped a picture of the text message while the screen was still lit up. She then hurried around the corner and enlarged the picture, her eyes blinking in surprise when she saw who the text was from: Evelyn Hall.

Why did Evelyn Hall need money? And whose phone had she been texting? Misty waited for a while, hoping someone would come from the back room to retrieve the phone. When she heard footsteps coming toward her from the stairwell, she quickly continued on her way to the kitchen before someone saw her and asked what she was doing.

After her visit to the kitchen, where Delta happily fixed her a plate of chicken salad, coleslaw, and potato salad, Misty decided to take her meal upstairs to eat. On the way to her room, she casually stopped by the front desk once again to find that the cell phone was no longer there.

CHAPTER 31

That evening at supper, excited chatter filled the dining room as everyone discussed the road finally getting cleared.

"I'll certainly be glad to go home," Evelyn stated with a sigh. "I'm so tired of not having any electricity."

"Yeah, I don't know if I'll be able to get used to not dining by candlelight after this," Luke said with a chuckle.

"It'll sure be nice to cook on a stove again," Delta said as she rolled their supper in on a cart. Merrick was following her with an electric lantern, and Misty thought they all looked like characters out of a medieval TV show.

"We've all sort of become family this week, though, haven't we?" Merrick asked with a smile. "I'm going to miss you all when you leave."

"Don't worry, brother, I'll still be here," Hudson teased as he clapped his brother-in-law on the back. It seemed the argument Misty and Brice had witnessed the day before had blown over.

They all filled their plates with chicken salad sandwiches left over from lunch, and grilled corn on the cob that Delta had cooked on the grill.

"If you've got to have leftovers, the least I can do is to make the side dish special," she told them all in her typical, boisterous fashion.

Everyone sat at a large, round table to eat, and Evelyn ended up next to Misty. With a slight smirk on her face, she leaned around to look at both Misty and Brice and asked, "What happened to you two last night? We all went to bed and y'all were still out in the woods."

Brice's face flushed, and Misty felt her temper bristle at the insinuation behind the question. "We made the mistake of going to Devil's Cliff and got stuck up there," Misty stated, turning to stare directly at Evelyn. "Isn't that where your friend was killed?"

Evelyn blinked, her own face beginning to flush red. "Uh, yes, it is. Whatever made you go up there?" She stammered.

"I read about your friend's accident and wanted to see the cliffs for myself," Misty replied, continuing to watch Evelyn closely. "The night he was killed, none of you heard anything or knew why he was at the cliffs?"

Evelyn stared down at her food, which she was now absently picking at, and shook her head. "No, I don't know why he was there," she replied. "We all assumed he couldn't sleep, decided to take a walk, and got turned around."

"He was raised in this area, wasn't he?" Misty pressed. "Don't you think it strange that he would get turned around?"

Evelyn shrugged. "I suppose so, but I guess we'll never know."

"Weren't the two of you dating?"

Evelyn's head jerked up, and she stared at Misty in surprise. "Who told you that?" She wanted to know.

Seeing that she'd apparently hit a nerve, Misty attempted to play it cool. "Someone around here mentioned it," she casually replied. "Perhaps it was Mr. Merrick when we were looking at his old photos? I really can't remember."

Her jaw tightening, Evelyn said coolly, "Jackson wanted to date me, but I wasn't really interested."

"I heard he and Terrence had a fight over you that night."

Her face had slowly begun to lose its color since the beginning of their conversation, and Evelyn now looked white as a ghost. Clearing her throat, she said tightly, "I don't remember much about that night. It was so long ago, you know."

With that being said, Evelyn politely turned away from Misty and began conversing with her husband. It was obvious she was finished with the conversation about Jackson's death, but Misty knew she wasn't telling the complete truth. There was something the group of friends had kept a secret about that night, and Misty felt she was finally beginning to put it all together.

After supper, everyone said good night, and Misty, Brice, and Luke went upstairs. Luke had been unusually quiet at supper, and Misty asked if anything was wrong.

"No, I'm just ready to get out of this place," he replied with a tight smile. "You two must be ready to get back home, right?"

They both nodded. "Yes, I am," Misty replied, adding with a laugh, "I really miss my dog."

"Well, as soon as those roads are cleared, I'm out of here," Luke said. "I'm even thinking of going on a vacation next week, maybe to the Bahamas or Mexico."

Brice raised his eyebrows in surprise. "Is your business doing so well that you can take off this whole week *and* next week?"

Luke glanced away and shrugged. "Yeah, I'm doing pretty good."

Before Brice could say anything further, Luke said good night and excused himself.

"He's more solemn tonight than usual, isn't he?" Misty asked once Luke's door was shut.

Brice nodded, his brow furrowed. "Yeah, it's not like him. I wonder where he was yesterday when you and I…well, when we went out to the falls."

At the sudden choked sound in Brice's voice, Misty looked up at him to see his cheeks flushing once again. She knew he was thinking of their kiss; she'd thought of it almost all day. She wondered if he'd really *wanted* to kiss her, or if she'd initiated the first move. She honestly couldn't remember. She wanted to ask him but was afraid of what his answer might be. If he said he'd never intended for it to happen, she wasn't certain she could ever face him again.

"Yeah, I wondered where he was, too," Misty said softly, glancing down at the toes of her shoes that were caught in the beam of her flashlight.

"Look, Misty…"

There was a cautious tone in Brice's voice, and Misty felt herself tense. Her mind went into panic mode, and she quickly began to back away from him.

"I'm really tired, Brice," she said, forcing herself to sound as normal as possible. "I'll see you in the morning, okay?"

His mouth still open from his interrupted speech, Brice simply nodded and said, "Yeah, sure. Good night."

Hurrying into her room and closing the door, Misty leaned against the solid wood for a moment. She listened as Brice hesitated in the hallway, as if uncertain of what had just happened, and then she heard his footsteps as he went into his own room and shut the door.

With a sigh, Misty pushed off the door and went out onto her balcony. Since the electricity had yet to be restored on the mountain, the night was as black as a raven's wings. Stars glittered from the sky, and the Milky Way was the most visible Misty had ever seen. As she leaned against the railing, her mind was reeling with thoughts and questions. She knew, or at least suspected, that Brice would broach the subject of their kiss again, and what would she say? She cared about him, and she'd felt something pass between them during those few hours on the cliff, but what did that mean exactly? She'd felt something when Adam kissed her, too.

At least you know Adam cares for you, she told herself.

Did Brice *not* care about her, though? She knew he did, at least as a friend. He was a mystery when it came to matters of the heart, though, and Misty couldn't be certain what this kiss had done to their friendship. What if things were never the same between them after this? She didn't want to think about that now. She was too tired.

Sitting down on the balcony's rocking chair, Misty pulled out her cell phone and opened the social media app. She was scrolling through everyone's photos and posts when a suggestion came up. Immediately recognizing Delta's name and photo, Misty clicked on her page and scrolled down to the last thing she'd posted. It was a photo of Merrick, Hudson, Frankie, Delta, Evelyn, and Caleb, taken last Saturday at the festival. Luke was standing to the side talking to someone at a nearby booth, but he wasn't taking an active part in the picture.

Something was niggling at Misty in the back of her mind, and she zoomed in on the photo to study it closely for a moment. She looked at each person, taking in the familiar faces and…wait, there it was! Her eyes widening, Misty sat up straighter and looked at the photo closer. It was pretty fuzzy, but Misty recognized it immediately. It was a turquoise bead, just like the one she'd found in Terrence's bathroom. She remembered it clearly now and quickly took a screenshot of the photo to show the sheriff tomorrow.

Misty sat back in the chair again and crossed her legs, her mind whirling. If she now knew where the bead came from, that could only mean one thing. She knew who the killer was.

CHAPTER 32

After her discovery, Misty barely slept all night. She tossed and turned, her mind refusing to stop and rest. When Saturday morning arrived bright and sunny, she dragged herself from bed and went downstairs.

"Whoa, you look tired," were Brice's first words when he spotted her. "Are you okay?"

"Not really," she replied. Glancing around to make certain no one was close enough to hear, she lowered her voice and said, "Brice, I think I know who…"

"Hey, are you two going to join us outside?"

Blinking at the sudden interruption, Misty turned to find Merrick poking his head in from the back door.

"We're having sort of a celebration," he added with a bright smile. "Since the road should be cleared anytime now, we decided to throw a last-minute party. Grab a plate from Delta at the grill and join us!"

Misty and Brice followed Merrick outside, where several quilts had been spread out in a circle along the grounds. Delta handed them a plate filled with freshly cut fruit, a crepe drizzled with chocolate and powdered sugar, and two pieces of crispy bacon.

"There's a pot of coffee on each quilt," she told them with a smile. "Enjoy."

There was a bouquet of flowers in the center of each quilt, and music played softly from a vintage record player nearby. A few colorful balloons, which appeared to have been left over from a previous party, were attached to a beautiful, old picnic basket in the midst of all the quilts. It was very charming, and Misty smiled at the apparent thoughtfulness behind the gesture.

"When did y'all do all of this?" Evelyn asked excitedly as she and Caleb joined the others.

"This morning," Frankie stated, her tone less than thrilled. "Merrick thought it would be a nice send-off for everyone."

"This is very nice, Merrick," Caleb said, nodding politely to their host. "Thank you."

Misty and Brice took one quilt, Caleb and Evelyn took another, and after a bit of coaxing, Hudson talked Frankie into joining them.

"When do we ever get the chance to have a picnic, honey?" he asked as he carried both their plates to the third quilt.

"Mrs. Delta, you should join us, too," Brice called out.

"Oh, no, I've got too much cleaning up to do," she told him. "There are a few extra crepes up here on this table if anyone wants seconds."

As Delta went inside, Luke emerged from the back door. He grabbed a plate and headed out into the yard, his hair a mess and his eyes a bit swollen.

"I guess I'll join you two," Luke stated as he sat with Misty and Brice.

Merrick joined Evelyn and Caleb, and Misty could hear them talking and laughing about old times. She could also hear the sound of the roadwork getting closer, and her stomach clenched nervously. What if the sheriff wouldn't listen to her? What if he accused her of interfering in a police investigation? Perhaps she should put the bead back where she'd found it and let him handle everything.

Suddenly, it hit her like a ton of bricks: she hadn't put Terrence's flash drive back where she'd found it! With everything that happened with Brice and Devil's Cliff, she'd forgotten all about it. If she didn't put it back now, while everyone was outside, she might not get another chance before the sheriff arrived.

Clearing her throat, Misty stood and excused herself, hoping no one suspected she was up to something. Delta was back on the porch cleaning the grill and straightening up as Misty climbed the wooden steps, and with a smile, she complimented her on the crepes and hurried inside.

The lodge was quiet as Misty ran up the stairs and into her room. With trembling fingers, she quickly put on the gloves and grabbed both the flash drive and the bead, still uncertain about whether to put the bead back.

I'll take it with me and decide once I'm safely

in the room, she thought.

For the third time in a week, Misty picked the lock to Terrence's room and slipped inside. She could hear everyone outside talking and laughing, but knew anyone could come upstairs at anytime and catch her. With a pounding heart, Misty opened the suitcase, found the toothbrush holder, and replaced the flash drive. She quickly closed the suitcase and stood there for a moment, deliberating about the bead. The sheriff had requested that no one enter the room until he arrived, but what if he overlooked the bead? Or what if it was spotted but simply thrown away as trash because they were convinced Terrence's death was an accident?

Before Misty could decide, the bedroom door suddenly swung open. With a gasp, Misty spun to find Terrence's killer standing in the doorway.

"What do you think you're doing?"

The blood left Misty's face at the same time the air fled from her lungs. She stood only about ten feet from the killer, who just happened to be blocking the only exit from the room. Misty didn't immediately feel threatened, however. Not yet, anyway. The eyes that stared back at her weren't hard or angry, but questioning, as if they weren't certain whether Misty knew they were the killer.

"I, uh…" Misty swallowed, struggling to think of an excuse for being in Terrence's room. Dare she try to talk her way out of it, or was it too late for that?

"Well?" the killer asked, raising an eyebrow. "How did you get in here?"

Misty took a deep breath and blew it out slowly. It was time to lay all the cards on the table; there was no use in pretending anymore. She didn't, however, want to spill everything all at once. Not until she could figure out a way to get out of this room.

"I picked the lock," she stated simply as her eyes slowly drifted around the room in search of a diversion or some sort of weapon. "I wanted the chance to see Terrence's room for myself before the police got here."

"Why is that?"

Misty lifted her chin as she turned her silver gaze back toward the killer. "Because I know his death wasn't an accident," she stated coolly.

"And how do you know that?" The killer asked, eyes narrowing.

Misty shrugged. "There are a lot of people here who disliked Terrence, so it seems obvious to me that murder isn't out of the question."

"That's not the only reason, though, is it?"

"No." Misty shook her head. "I know that some would blame the death on the black wolf, but I heard someone coming from Terrence's room that night. I didn't know who it was at the time or what they were doing, but when Terrence turned up dead the next morning, it wasn't hard to figure out."

Misty suddenly thought of the flash drive then.

Could that work as a diversion? Could she convince the killer to walk over to the suitcase, which might give Misty the chance to make a run for it?

"You didn't simply come in here today to poke around and we both know it." The killer's voice had taken on a darker tone, and when the door was suddenly pushed closed, Misty realized with a sinking stomach that it would be much more difficult to escape now. "You broke into his room to return something, and I want to know what."

"What do you think I could have found?" Misty asked innocently.

"It's time to stop pretending, Miss Raven. You found something that you and I both know will prove *I* murdered Terrence."

CHAPTER 33

Misty slowly began to back away, her eyes never leaving Delta Coffey's. She'd figured out that Delta was the murderer last night, but hearing it spoken from the killer's very own lips was another thing in itself.

"How did you know I found something?" Misty asked, hoping she could keep Delta talking long enough that someone would come inside looking for them.

"After you nearly caught me out in the hallway that night, I knew you would suspect Terrence was murdered," Delta said. "So, I've been keeping an eye on you. When I saw you come up here just now, I knew you were up to something. You found the bead from my earring, didn't you?"

"I actually didn't know the bead belonged to you until last night," Misty told her. "I only saw you wear the earring once, so I couldn't remember where I'd seen that particular bead. I saw a picture of you from the festival on social media last night, and that's when it finally clicked. What happened, Delta? Why did you kill Terrence? Because of your sister?"

Her face tight, Delta nodded stiffly. "Yes," she whispered hoarsely. "If not for him, my sister never would have killed herself. I **hated** that man, and when he suddenly showed back up all these years later and started causing more problems, I knew I needed to rid the world of his nauseating presence.”

“And what about the bead I found in the linen closet with the blood on it?” Misty asked. “Did you go into the bathroom for a towel? How did it end up in there?”

“When I struck Terrence on the head, blood splattered all over me,” Delta said with a disgusted look on her face. “I ran into the bathroom to grab a towel, and when I threw open the closet door, it caught the earring and tore it from my ear. It fell to the floor and broke apart. I knew I was missing a bead, but couldn’t find it.” Reaching her hand out, Delta said, “Give it to me now, please. I don’t want to hurt you; I simply want the bead so I can destroy it.”

“You mean you’ll let me live, even though I know the truth?” Misty asked, her eyes narrowing.

“It’ll be my word against yours, honey, and everyone around here will support me,” Delta stated. “Now hurry up and give it to me.”

Misty backed away and shook her head. “I’m afraid I can’t do that, Delta.”

Sighing, Delta slowly pulled a knife from her apron pocket and said, “I guess you leave me no choice then.”

When Delta started toward her, Misty shoved the suitcase at the older, much larger woman and dove into the bathroom. She quickly slammed the door shut and locked it, her stomach sinking at how high the frosted window was over the bathtub.

"This old lock won't hold long, Miss Raven," Delta said from the other side of the door. "Why don't you just give up now instead of dragging this out?"

Misty could hear Delta starting to pick at the lock, and with her heart in her throat, she climbed on top of the bathtub rim and stretched up toward the window. It didn't have a latch with which to open it and Misty couldn't see out, but she knew it faced the backyard. Snatching off her gloves, she began frantically rapping on the glass in the hope that someone would hear her and come to investigate.

"They can't hear you over the sound of the roadwork," Delta said, the doorknob continuing to wiggle.

"If you kill me, Delta, everyone will know," Misty called out as she grabbed the heavy soap dish and began banging more forcefully against the window. "You won't be able to cover this up, too."

"I'll make it look like *you* killed Terrence and then committed suicide," Delta said just as the bathroom door swung open. Her eyes were angry and her face red, and Misty knew she was trapped.

Delta lunged across the bathroom toward her, the knife poised to kill. Her heart pounding, Misty threw the soap dish as hard as she could, but it only bounced off Delta's shoulder. With a sharp cry at the unexpected blow, Delta paused, giving Misty a split second to let out an ear-piercing scream. There was no way she could get around the larger woman, but if only someone would hear her, perhaps she could still be saved.

With a grunt, Delta glared at Misty and took another menacing step forward. Looking around frantically for yet another object to defend herself with, Misty's heart sank when she found nothing. This was it; there was nothing she could do to save herself.

Just as Delta lunged at Misty, the knife raised high in the air, a deep voice called out sharply from the bedroom.

"Delta, what on earth is going on?"

Delta froze just as Merrick hurried into the bathroom, his eyes wide, and Misty slowly sank down the wall to sit on the bathtub rim. Her legs were shaking violently and her heart pounded so viciously that she feared she might faint.

"Miss Raven tried to attack me," Delta said, looking frazzled. "I was only protecting myself."

With a look of disbelief, Merrick shook his head and said, "I heard what you said, Delta. **You** killed Terrence and were going to make Misty look like she did it. How could you?"

Misty watched as Delta deflated like a balloon at the disappointment and shock in Merrick's voice. She dropped the knife, and with shaking hands, covered her face as she began to cry.

"I'm so sorry, Mr. Merrick," she sobbed. "I couldn't help but kill him after what he did to my sister and with what he was trying to do to all of you. Please don't hate me, Mr. Merrick. I don't think I could bear it if you did."

"Merrick, what is going on? We could all hear some sort of commotion from outside. What's wrong with Delta?"

Misty peered around the bathroom door to see that Frankie, Hudson, and the rest of the guests had come upstairs as well. Frankie had voiced the question, her forehead wrinkled in confusion as she stared at Delta.

"Misty, are you okay?" Brice asked, hurrying past everyone when he saw Misty huddled against the corner.

Misty nodded and stood up to lean against Brice when he put his arm around her. Turning to look at Frankie, she answered the question directed at Merrick.

"Delta killed Terrence, and she was trying to kill me, too," Misty stated.

Everyone gasped, and Brice's hold on Misty tightened. Merrick bent to pick up the knife Delta had dropped, his expression pained as he glanced uncertainly at their longtime cook and friend.

"I wasn't really going to kill you," Delta said, sniffling. "I just wanted to scare you into giving me that bead."

At the questioning look on everyone's faces, Misty pulled the bagged bead from her pocket and held it up.

"I found this in Terrence's linen closet," she said. "It's a bead that fell from Delta's earring, and it has Terrence's blood on it."

"Delta, you really killed him?" Hudson asked, his face ashen.

"He destroyed my sister, and he was trying to destroy your family," Delta snapped as she turned to glare at Hudson. "Can you blame me?"

"How was Terrence destroying our family?" Merrick wanted to know.

When Delta didn't answer, Misty spoke up and said, "He needed money after his divorce, and when he found out who killed Jackson Dagon, he came home to blackmail Jackson's killer."

"What?" Merrick asked, his brow furrowed. "Jackson's death was an accident, Misty."

"No, it wasn't." Turning to look at Jackson's killer, she raised an eyebrow and asked, "Was it, Frankie?"

Frankie's face lost all its color, and for an instant, Misty thought she might turn and bolt from the room. After a moment, as everyone was staring at her in shock, she cleared her throat and said stiffly, "I don't know what you're talking about."

Misty eased past Delta, who leaned against the bathroom counter still sniffling, and went into the bedroom. Pointing to the suitcase, she said, "It's all in there, Frankie. Terrence and Evelyn were having an affair, and one night when Evelyn apparently had too much to drink, she spilled the beans on your little secret. The problem was, she didn't know Terrence was recording the whole thing."

As Misty spoke, she heard Evelyn gasp softly. Turning to look at the Halls, she saw Evelyn was white as a ghost and Caleb's jaw was clenched tightly.

"You know a little about blackmail, don't you, Evelyn?" Misty asked. "You've been doing it to Frankie for years."

"I have not," Evelyn hissed, her ashen face turning red. "I *never* blackmailed Frankie."

Frankie began to laugh then, the humorless guffaw echoing loudly throughout the room. Shaking her head, she glared at Evelyn in disgust.

"You never actually threatened to turn me in to the police," she spat, "but I know you, Evelyn. I know you would have turned me in if I didn't give you what you wanted."

Sniffing, Evelyn raised her chin indignantly and said, "I only ever told you I needed a bit of money on a few occasions, or that I wanted to go shopping. I never said anything about you killing Jackson. It was your guilty conscience that made you pay for anything I ever asked for."

"Frankie, you actually *killed* him?" Merrick asked, his face a mask of shock.

"It was an accident," she snapped. "I heard him tell Evelyn to meet him on the cliff at midnight, and when I saw him leave his tent early, I followed him up there." Her lips were curled in disdain, and her normally sour expression was filled with hatred and disgust. "He'd said that he loved *me,* but then he started ignoring me and giving all of his attention to Evelyn. So, I went up on that cliff after him and gave him a piece of my mind. I told him I still loved him, but do you know what he did? He looked at me with pity and said I needed to move on, that he didn't care for me in that way anymore. When he turned his back on me, I got angry and pushed him. I wasn't trying to kill him! I didn't even realize how close he was to the edge."

The whole time Frankie talked, Hudson stood there silently. At first, Misty thought he was just in a state of shock, but by the expression on his face, she realized he'd known all along.

"You knew, didn't you, Hudson?" Misty asked.

Hudson nodded. "Frankie broke down one night about two weeks after it happened and told me everything. She said since it was an accident, there was no need to tell the police, so I agreed." Looking at his wife with love and warmth in his eyes, he said softly, "I didn't care that she loved Jackson. All I wanted was her. Why didn't you tell me about the blackmail, honey?"

When Hudson asked the question, he reached for Frankie, but she moved out of his reach and turned away from him.

"There was nothing that could be done about it," she stated simply. "I knew it was just a burden I was going to have to bear."

Eyeing his sister suspiciously, Merrick asked,

"Where did you get the money, though? I've seen the results of some of your and Evelyn's shopping trips. You don't make enough money to pay for all of that."

Avoiding Merrick's gaze, Frankie glanced down at the floor, her stony expression tightening with guilt. "I borrowed it from the lodge," she said in a low voice. "Since I'm the one who handles the books, I knew y'all wouldn't find out. I intended to put it back gradually when I could, but Evelyn constantly wanted more money and my borrowing got out of hand."

With a hard expression, Merrick looked at Evelyn and asked, "How could you do this? I thought you were my sister's friend."

Evelyn looked at her husband for support, but he simply stared coldly back at her. With a sigh, Evelyn said, "Would you have rather I told the sheriff what I saw? I was there, standing in the trees when she pushed him. It may have not been intentional, but she still killed him."

"Blackmail is also a crime," Hudson snapped angrily.

"Which is what Terrence was trying to do to you, too, right?" Misty asked Evelyn. "You'd broken off the affair, but he wasn't finished with you yet. He came here with two agendas: to blackmail both you and Frankie. Did he threaten to tell Caleb if you insisted on ending it with him? Or did he tell you about the recording and say he'd turn you in for blackmail?"

"Caleb already knew about the affair," Evelyn stated with a sniff. "So, yes, Terrence threatened to turn me in for blackmail."

"We've got to tell the sheriff all of this when he arrives," Merrick said, running his fingers through his hair.

"I don't want to go to prison, Merrick," Frankie said, backing away from her brother.

"You said it was an accident, Frankie," Merrick told her. "We can't continue to keep this a secret. And Delta," he said, turning to the older woman, "as much as I hate to turn you in, what you did was wrong. You're going to have to tell the sheriff."

Just then, they all heard the sound of cars approaching. Within a few seconds, the front door to the lodge was opened and a loud voice called out, "Where is everyone?"

CHAPTER 34

T he rest of the day passed in a frenzy of confessions, tears, statements, and the gathering of evidence. The sheriff took both Delta and Frankie down to the police station, and after they'd left, Merrick told Evelyn she would have to pay back all the money she'd taken or he'd turn her in for blackmail.

One question Misty posed to Evelyn before she and Caleb left was why Terrence left Dahlonega all those years ago and never came back. Misty had originally assumed it had something to do with Jackson's death, but since he hadn't known any of the details until recently, she couldn't figure out what made him leave.

"He assaulted a girl that used to live up the mountain," Evelyn told her. "The girl's father told him to get out of town or he'd kill him."

"Why didn't the man just tell the sheriff?" Misty wanted to know.

Evelyn shrugged. "He probably didn't want the sheriff to know he was making illegal moonshine up at his place."

While Evelyn and Caleb left Saturday night, Misty and Brice decided to stay at the lodge and go home the next morning. Luke went home, as well, after getting a promise that they'd stop by his house on the way out to get the pictures and letters his mom had saved.

The next morning, after packing and loading Brice's truck with their suitcases, Misty went back inside to check out. Merrick was at the front desk, looking absolutely exhausted, and her heart clenched at what he was going through. She couldn't imagine how he must feel to have discovered after all these years that his sister was responsible for his friend's death and then took money from the lodge to guarantee Evelyn's silence. She also knew he was hurt over what Delta did; she'd been at the lodge for so long that she was like family. Misty knew he must be feeling pretty blindsided by everything.

"Well, Miss Raven, your stay turned out to be much different from what you'd imagined, didn't it?" Merrick asked as he took her room key.

Misty smiled softly at him. "Yes, it certainly did. In some odd way, though, I enjoyed it…minus the attempt on my life there at the end."

Merrick sighed and shook his head. "I'm so sorry about that."

"Don't worry. It's not the first time someone has tried to kill me," Misty replied with a shrug.

"Well, I certainly hope you'll visit us again sometime," Merrick told her kindly.

Hesitating, Misty eyed Merrick for a moment, wondering if she dared ask the question in her heart. She'd come to like Merrick, and she didn't want to make him any more upset than he already was.

"Mr. Merrick," she said softly as she finagled with the receipt he'd given her, "you know why I came here in the first place, and I'm…I'm just wondering if you could answer a rather direct question for me?"

Tilting his head, Merrick said, "Of course, I will. What is it, Miss Raven?"

Taking a deep breath, her heart pounding loudly in her ears, Misty asked, "Are…are you by any chance my father?"

Merrick blinked, and Misty felt her face flush. Why had she been so direct? She could have tried to ask it a little more gently, but she needed to know for sure, and just straight out asking him was the only thing she knew to do. In some way, she wished he'd say yes. He'd known her mother and had been one of her closest friends, and Misty felt a connection with him because of that. He was also a good man with a kind heart. Who wouldn't want someone like that for a father?

"I honestly wish I could say yes," Merrick said with a sad smile, "but no. I'm not your father, Misty."

Her eyes filling with tears, Misty nodded and glanced down at her hands, feeling disappointed and also embarrassed. When Merrick reached out and put his large hand over hers, she forced herself to look at him again.

"I was in love with your mother," he said softly,

"but she didn't feel the same about me. Whomever the man was that she finally let into her heart must have been very special, and I hope you find him someday soon. God bless you, Misty Raven."

With a wobbly smile, Misty thanked him and went outside to join Brice in his truck. He'd known she was going to ask Merrick, and when he saw the tears in her eyes, he didn't have to ask her how it went.

"Maybe Luke will have the answers you're looking for," was all he said as he reached for her hand.

As they pulled away from the lodge and began the trek down the mountain, Misty stared out the window, her mind as blurry as the trees that whirled by. Would she ever find her real father? She hoped Brice was right and that the letters and photographs Luke had would hold some answers, but at this point, she feared to keep hoping.

Just then, there was a break in the trees, and a large, rocky cliff could be seen from Misty's window. She looked at the very top of the cliff and blinked, her senses coming alive as she sat up straighter in her seat. At the top of the cliff, a black wolf stood tall and proud. It seemed to be looking right at Misty, its eyes steady and searching, as if it could see right into her very soul. Before she could call the wolf to Brice's attention, a group of trees suddenly blocked her view. When the cliff came back into sight seconds later, the wolf was gone.

The drive down the mountain was a quiet one. Misty said nothing to Brice about the wolf; she was starting to wonder if it had really been there in the first place. When they finally reached Luke's house, she'd convinced herself it was just her imagination.

"Here you go," Luke said as he came out to the truck, carrying a small box filled with photos and letters. "I hope this helps, Misty."

As Brice put the box in the truck, Misty gave Luke a hug and said, "Thank you, Luke. Whether I find what I'm looking for in that box or not, I'll have more of my mother than I did before."

Pulling back, Luke smiled down at Misty. With a sparkle in the depths of his black eyes, he said, "May the spirit of the wolf be with you, Misty Raven."

Tilting her head in confusion, Misty asked, "The spirit of death?"

Luke laughed. "No," he replied, shaking his head. "That's Ayohuhisdi, the black wolf here in these mountains. Other wolves are considered by my ancestors to represent courage, success, and perseverance."

Misty could see Luke's necklace poking from beneath his shirt, its beads glistening brightly in the morning sun. As he spoke, she could almost feel his grandfather's wise spirit with them, and she smiled.

"Thank you, Luke," she said, giving his hand a warm squeeze.

"Y'all drive safe, okay?" He told them, clapping Brice on the back. "And come see me again soon."

They waved goodbye, and the entire drive home, Misty looked through the pictures from Luke and read the letters out loud. The photos held no answers; they were simply happy, smiling images of Elena and Luke's mother. Misty didn't begrudge that fact, though. She was happy to have as many pictures of her mother as possible. The letters, too, didn't seem to hold much information; they were mostly about Vega, which was Misty's original name, and Karson. When she reached the last letter, however, the very first line caught Misty's attention.

"My mom wrote this letter right after she and Karson moved to Shady Pines," Misty said, her brow wrinkling as she scanned over the soft, slanted handwriting. "Brice, listen to this: *I saw him today, Nita. It's been three years, and I saw him! I had no idea I'd ever see him again; it caught me so off guard. I didn't tell Karson because I was afraid he might confront him. He recognized me and looked as shocked as I felt, but he was with another woman and didn't speak. The woman wasn't the same one he was previously engaged to, which also surprised me. If I see him again and he tries to talk to me, what do I say? I love Karson; he's been so good to me and my sweet girl, but I'll*

Misty lowered the letter and looked at Brice with wide eyes. "His name was Ricky," she breathed. Looking back down at the letter, she felt yet another spark of hope. There was no mention of a last name, but at least she had a bit of something to go on.

"That's wonderful, Misty," Brice said with a smile. "So, she saw him in Shady Pines?"

Misty shrugged. "I guess so, but she doesn't actually say that anywhere. Do you think he lived there? Do you know anyone named Ricky?"

Brice shook his head. "I can't think of anyone, but my aunt and uncle would probably know."

They weren't far from home now, and Misty wiggled in her seat with anticipation. Perhaps she really would find her father after all.

CHAPTER 35

onday morning when Misty woke up, she lay in bed for a while, happy to be home. She'd seen Tori the night before when she picked up Wally and knew her friend would be coming over to talk soon. Misty had just gotten up and fixed Wally's breakfast when she heard the front door open.

"I brought fresh muffins," Tori announced as soon as she entered the kitchen.

"Ooh, are they the orange ones I like so much?" Misty asked excitedly as she peered into the container.

"Of course," Tori replied with a smile as she helped herself to a cup of coffee. After making herself comfortable on one of the barstools, she put her chin in her hand and said, "Okay, tell me everything."

For the next hour, Misty relayed the story of her week at Black Wolf Lodge. Hearing it all spoken out loud made it seem like she was reading a script from an old film noir. She told Tori everything; the legend of the black wolf, the storm, Terrence's death, and finding his killer. She even included the unexpected kiss with Brice.

Her eyes widening with excitement over the

latter part, Tori exclaimed, "Misty! You really kissed? Oh, I'm over the moon. When's the wedding?"

Laughing, Misty shook her head and said, "Slow down there. Brice and I haven't even talked about it yet. In fact, I don't think he intended for it to happen and I have a feeling he's going to apologize for it."

With a frown, Tori absently stirred her coffee and said, "That doesn't make any sense. He cares for you, Misty. Anybody can see that. So, why would he apologize for kissing you?"

Misty shrugged. "Maybe because he's afraid of relationships? I don't know." With a sigh, Misty grabbed another muffin and said, "But anyway, tell me about your week. How is Mr. Neil?"

"He's going to be in the hospital for at least another week, and the doctor has already started him on physical therapy," Tori said. "He's got a long road of recovery ahead of him, but I'm just so thankful he's alive."

Tori hesitated then, and Misty got the feeling she wasn't telling her something. Touching her friend on the arm, Misty asked, "What's wrong, Tori? Did something else happen while we were gone?"

Chewing on her bottom lip, Tori slowly nodded her head. "When I came by your house that first night to see about Wally, I…I was attacked, Misty."

Misty felt the blood drain from her face. "By *Wally?*" She nearly screeched.

Hearing the sound of his name, Wally quickly sat up and looked at his owner questioningly.

"No, no," Tori immediately said, shaking her head. "Wally didn't attack me."

Taking a deep breath, Tori launched into the story of the stove repairman and Julian Cooper. As she spoke, Misty felt herself getting more and more upset. By the end of the story, she felt sick to her stomach.

"Oh, Tori, this is awful," she breathed. "What is being done about it?"

Tori fiddled with the handle on her coffee cup and said, "The police have been searching for Cooper, but they haven't had any luck finding him yet. I'm hoping he's long gone by now."

"Me, too," Misty replied with a sigh. Eyeing her friend, she said, "Look, why don't you stay with me for a few days? At least until we're more sure that Cooper is gone."

"I hate to impose…"

"Tori, how many times have I imposed on you?" Misty asked, raising an eyebrow. "Besides, this will sort of be like that girl trip we missed out on. We can stay up late and watch movies and eat popcorn."

"Well, I actually would prefer not to stay by myself just yet, so I think I'll take you up on your offer," Tori finally agreed. "I've got to go to the shop now, so I'll see you later this evening." Standing, Tori wrapped her arms around Misty's neck and gave her a quick hug. "You're the best, you know that? See you later!"

Tori

Later that afternoon, Tori closed the shop and was in her kitchen preparing dough for the following day when Brice knocked on the back door.

"Hey, how's my favorite cousin?" he asked, giving her a hug.

"You're here to play bodyguard, aren't you?" she asked, pinching his arm.

Brice smiled and shrugged sheepishly. "Pops told me what happened. Are you okay?"

Tori nodded. "I'm better than I was a few days ago. I'm going to stay with Misty for a little while until I feel more comfortable staying by myself."

"I think that's a great idea," Brice said, snitching a handful of chocolate chips from the bowl she had measured out.

Slapping at his hand, Tori eyed her cousin and said, "Speaking of Misty, when are you going to talk to her?"

Brice glanced away, avoiding her gaze, and she was positive he was blushing. "Talk to her about what?" he asked nonchalantly.

Frowning, Tori planted her hands on her hips and said, "You know about what, Brice Barlow. She told me about the kiss."

Yep, he was definitely blushing.

"I started to say something when we were back at the lodge, but she changed the subject," he told her, crossing his arms defensively.

"So try again," she stated drolly.

Brice didn't say anything for a moment, and Tori gave him his space to think while she kneaded the dough. He was leaning against her counter, slowly chewing on the chocolate chips, and there was a faraway look in his eyes that told Tori he was deep in thought.

"I don't exactly know what to say," he finally said, his voice low.

"You could start by telling her how you feel."

Brice looked over at his cousin, tilting his head as he asked, "And how do you think I feel?"

Wiping her hands on a nearby towel, Tori went to stand next to Brice. She looked him straight in the eye and said, "We were raised together, Brice. You're more like a brother than a cousin, and I can see right through that protective wall you keep firmly built around yourself." She gently rested her hand on his arm, her voice soft as she continued, "You care a great deal for Misty; I can see that as plainly as I see this green shirt you're wearing. Why don't you tell her, Brice? What is it that's holding you back?"

Brice sighed, his eyes filled with a war of emotions. "I'm afraid of getting my heart broken again," he said, glancing away to look down at the floor. "Misty is…well, she's like the wind. She's been through a lot, and her natural instinct is to pick up and blow away when things get tough, to not have any roots to tie her down. What if we gave it a chance, and she decided someday that she didn't want to be tied to *me* any longer?"

"Brice, she's been here for months now," Tori told him. "She has roots here whether she wants to admit it or not, and she's already told me she plans to stay here in Shady Pines. I really believe she cares for you, too, if you'll both just give it a shot."

Brice hesitated, as if he wanted to say something else, but didn't quite know how. Finally, he looked down at Tori and asked, "What about Adam? Doesn't she care for him, too?"

Tori blinked, caught off guard by the question. After a moment, she shrugged and said softly, "If I know her as well as I think I do, you're the one she wants to be with. But I guess that's a question you'll just have to ask Misty."

Brice nodded and stood there silently chewing on the chocolate chips for several moments, his gaze pointed toward the ground. "You're right," he finally said, his voice filling with resolve. "I do need to talk to her. Maybe I'll go see her now. Unless you're about to head that way? If so, I can wait until tomorrow."

Tori smiled and shook her head. "No, I've got to go home first and pack my bags." Squeezing his arm, she said, "Good luck, Brice."

As she watched him go, Tori felt nervous and anxious for them both. What if she'd pushed Brice into talking things out with Misty, only for him to end up hurt again? She didn't think Misty would reject him, but as Brice had said, Misty was different and not always an easy person to figure out.

Tori had just finished putting the dough in the refrigerator when her cell phone chimed. Checking to see who the message was from, she was surprised to find that it was from Pops.

"Can you come to the store? I need your help with something."

Confused, Tori asked him what he needed her help with, but he never answered. Supposing he must be too busy to answer or call, Tori hurriedly packed up her things and headed to the hardware store.

When Tori arrived at the store, she used her key and went in through the front door. Surprised to find that the lights were turned off, Tori called out to Pops, but he never answered. She could see a light shining from the back, so she closed the door behind her and slowly made her way through the store.

Tori had spent many hours in this place, from playing with the tools as a child to helping run the cash register as a teenager. This store held a lot of good memories for her, but for some reason, the way the shadows played along the aisles and the huge shelves towered forebodingly above her head made Tori feel oddly uncomfortable. There was no sound other than her heels clicking against the linoleum floor, and Tori suddenly wondered why Pops would ask her for help instead of Brice.

She reached the back room and slowly pushed the door open, warning bells sounding in her mind when Pops still didn't answer her. She stood in the doorway for a moment, pondering whether to call Brice, when she heard a moan coming from the other side of her grandfather's desk. Hurrying around the antique, mahogany workspace, Tori gasped when she saw Pops lying on the floor with a bloody gash on his head.

Before she could rush to his side, a gloved hand snaked around from behind and pressed a damp cloth over her mouth and nose. Everything Dylan taught her flew through her mind all at once like an explosion of confetti. She tried to jerk away, to elbow and kick at the large body behind her, but it was of no use. The moves Dylan had taught her couldn't help in overcoming such brute strength, especially since she'd been so unsuspecting and he'd gotten the drop on her. The chloroform was beginning to take effect as the room began to spin wildly around her. Within just a few moments, Tori slumped to the floor, unconscious.

CHAPTER 36

Misty

After Tori had left that morning, Misty went outside and spent some time with Wally. She'd missed him while she was gone and could tell he was happy to have her home. They played fetch, hide-and-seek, and even went for a trek in the woods. When they went back inside, Misty began working on the upstairs renovations. By the time she looked at her phone, it was almost five o'clock, and she was starving. She put a chicken pot pie from the market into the oven, and while she waited for it to cook, she sat at the kitchen table and read over her mother's letters again.

"My mother mentioned that Ricky was previously engaged," Misty said to Wally, who tilted his head as she talked to him. "I wonder what she meant by that."

Just then, it hit her that she hadn't checked her emails in over a week; perhaps the DNA website had contacted her with results by now. Feeling a little nervous, Misty opened the email app on her phone to find that an email had arrived in her inbox just that morning from the website. Her heart pounding, Misty opened the email to find a message which read: ***"We have found a fifty percent DNA match for you! Click the link below to see the results."***

Misty stared at the e-mail for a moment in shock. Fifty percent? That meant the website had matched her with a parent, and since Elena was dead, that could only mean one thing. The website had found her father.

Her heart pounding, Misty moved her thumb down to tap on the link but paused when she suddenly heard the sound of an approaching vehicle. Thinking that it was Tori, she stood and hurried through the house to share the news with her friend just as the pounding of footsteps racing onto the porch met her ears. Before she could reach the front door, it was flung open and Brice nearly ran her over in his haste to get inside. His face was white and his eyes were wide with panic as he grabbed her arms to steady her when she stumbled back.

"Brice, what on earth is the matter?" she asked.

Trying to catch his breath, Brice panted, "It-it's Tori. Misty, she's been kidnapped."

<u>A NOTE FROM THE AUTHOR</u>

Thank you so much for reading book #3 of "A Shady Pines Mystery" series. If you enjoyed it, please leave a review on Amazon or Goodreads – or both! I look forward to hearing from you. Also, if you're interested in receiving news of upcoming books, discounts, free e-books, and more, please sign up for my newsletter at:
https://newsletter.jennyelaineauthor.com/